THE THORN

First paperback edition April 2022

Cover design by Onur Burc

ISBN 979-8-9858041-0-2 (paperback)
ISBN 979-8-9858041-1-9 (ebook)

Published by Beyond Summit Press
www.josephnoll.com

To my mother,
Elaine, and father,
Mike, for whom I cannot live without.

Table of Contents

THE THORN

Joseph Noll

Prologue

Twelve of them were standing around the long wooden table. They weren't human, far from it. These beings were from a hostile race, one that doesn't forge alliances but sees enemies everywhere.

Eight feet tall, these beefy creatures had thick gray skin and eyes so dark they were like miniature black holes, sucking in all the light around them. They all wore the same armor, impenetrable by anything that wasn't made of the same material. A meeting of some kind was taking place, although not much was being said.

The creature at the head of the table stood taller than the already eight-foot creatures. The massive medallion around his neck bore symbols of another alien race. A memento of his victory, along with the scars all over his face and his biceps from another war he'd won.

The leader.

The room was dimly lit by ceiling lanterns, and the shadows fell on the benches with dashboards and the thousands of buttons on them. The metal walls constantly shook as if in sync with the light flashing from the button on the table. Something was happening. Everyone was staring at their leader expectantly, ready to hear his plan. The leader grinned, and two bottom fangs appeared over his upper lip. He was ready to show them what he had been planning.

The leader lifted his massive arm and pushed the button on the table. Suddenly the entire table dispensed a dark blue light, illuminating the whole room as a panel in the far wall slid open, revealing an enormous window. Outside the window, something was approaching. Or were they approaching it instead? A perfectly round object came into view. It had many vibrant shades of blue and green, as well as other less distinct shades of white and black.

Murmurs filled the room. The eleven others were stunned, but at the same time, confident and ready. For it wasn't just any object, but a planet filled with beautiful mountains and vast oceans. A planet that had intelligent life of its own.

The Earth.

Chapter One

Lylon

I've always considered my life like a stereotypical movie. I'm the valedictorian in my senior class, never making below a 95 in all AP courses. While others around me struggle, I never do. I love playing video games and making out with my hot girlfriend, Valerie. It still surprises me to this day that we're together because I never thought I'd meet someone perfect for me. How we met, though, was a complete coincidence.

Three years ago, her family moved here from Boulder, Colorado. On her first day at school, I happened to be in the office when they made her schedule, and the counselor handed it to me and asked me to show her around the school.

"Hey, I'm Lylon Porter," I had said, stumbling on my words. She looked at me with her luminous green eyes, and that was it. Her blonde hair fell on her back in soft curls, and she wore jeans with a red and black flannel long-sleeve shirt. I could feel my body start to sweat. She looked puzzled for a moment but smiled and shook my hand.

"Lylon? Interesting name. I'm Valerie Ray," she said as we left the office.

I nodded. "So, Colorado, huh? What made you leave such a nice place and come somewhere boring?"

She laughed. "I didn't want to leave. My dad's job forced us to move. He works in finance for a private company, and they moved locations. The move came with a pay raise, so there wasn't really an option."

Her first-period class had come into view, and I was disappointed that we wouldn't get to talk any longer. I handed her schedule to her, and she smiled.

"Well, Valerie, I hope you like it here. It isn't that bad."

"Thanks, Lylon. You know, it's a cool name. I like it," she said before entering her class.

If I hadn't been in the office that day to deliver the attendance sheet, I wouldn't have met her. The timing was perfect.

Later that day, she found me at lunch sitting by myself, so she sat down next to me. Since I had welcomed her, she didn't want me to eat alone. We ended up being late for our next class because we kept talking about our likes and dislikes. We both liked *Nirvana*, loved to binge-watch *The Fresh Prince of Bel-Air*, and were crazy about action movies. We were sent to the office for being late, but I couldn't bring myself to regret any of that. That day felt like a dream.

A week later, we started dating.

That all happened in September of freshman year. Now it's October of senior year, and we need to start thinking about what we want to do with our lives. We could get into just about any college we want, but we want to travel and see the world. We want to be together. I think my parents will be happy wherever I end up as long as I'm happy. I'm surprised they haven't tried to sway me toward a specific career, considering that my parents have done so well.

My mom, Liza, is a nurse at East Dallas Medical Center, and she saves lives on a daily basis. I'm proud that she's my mom. She puts her intelligence to use every day, and she always looks out for others before herself. I have no idea how she manages to be so selfless all of the time. It's like an obsession with her. She claims it's because she has to, but I don't know if I believe that. The truth is that helping others makes her happy. I only wish I could be more like her.

That's also the main reason my dad fell in love with her. Mom is very pretty and gets compliments all the time. She's above average in height, with black hair past her shoulders and hazel eyes. But my dad sees past her beauty and loves her gentle nature and caring personality. He often says that her looks are just a bonus. Some people don't believe him, but I do because Dad never lies.

Everyone says that I take after my dad, Travis. At six-two, with short black hair and brown eyes, he wears glasses, not because he needs them, but because he says they make him look more sophisticated. When he was young, he lived in a small town in the middle of Texas and attended a small school of roughly a hundred kids. He always got a perfect score on his standardized tests and was accepted to Harvard, majoring in computer science. After his graduation, he got a job in the IT department at East Dallas Medical Center. My mom was a summer intern at the same hospital, and that's how they met. They wanted to travel and see the world, but then Mom got pregnant with me and they got married and settled down in Dallas.

I have always thought of leaving after graduation to live the dream life my parents wanted, but I also feel like I need to do something to make them proud. My parents have sacrificed so much for me that I could never repay them. The only thing I can do is be the best me.

Little did I know, though, that the world would change very soon and need more people like my mom. I was soon to find out that life is full of selfish choices. It took me losing almost everything over the next three days to figure out which choices I was willing to make, and the price I would have to pay.

Chapter Two

Day One

Today is a very cool October morning, and the leaves have finally started to change on the trees. It gets later and later every year. I remember when the leaves would change in August ten years ago. Not anymore, though. One of mankind's flaws, global warming, is to be blamed for that.

It's so early in the morning that the sun hasn't risen yet. But I have to get up early today. I don't usually get up until 8 a.m. because I don't have a first period, so my first class starts at 9 a.m. But today, I'm going in early to work on a robotics project with the nerds. Even though I don't hang with the nerds outside of school, I consider myself to be one.

The colorful trees pass by as I sit in the passenger seat of my dad's car. He's driving me today because my car is in the shop. My parents bought me a car when I turned sixteen, but I didn't expect it to be a piece of junk that only cost a grand. A 2002 Saturn. Thanks, guys.

I wonder how Valerie would react if I drove to school in a brand-new car. To be honest, I don't think she would care because she doesn't care about money.

"Lylon!"

"What?! Sorry," I reply, startled.

"I've called your name like eight times, bud. You need to get your hearing checked?" my dad asks with a grin.

"No. We both know my hearing is like twenty times better than yours! I've just got a lot on my mind."

Dad chuckles. "You're thinking about Valerie again, aren't you? You don't have to deny it. I know that look."

"You should be looking at the road… and yeah, I was."

"I knew it!" Dad says triumphantly. "So, when are you going to ask her to prom?"

I roll my eyes. "Dad, for like the hundredth time, prom is at the end of the year, and homecoming is at the beginning. We decided not to go to homecoming because it's always so boring it's like watching paint dry."

Dad looks thoughtful. "Well, why don't you two go out anyway. Say, instead of going to the dance, you do something else. That way, you won't be bored at home."

"That's actually a good idea," I say, deep in thought.

Dad smiles again. "See? I still have some good ideas in this old brain of mine!"

"Yeah, I guess."

"You know what else is a good idea?" Dad asks.

"What?"

"Doing your chores when you get home."

"Ugh, Dad! I don't have time. I have this project and a lot of other AP homework to do. Can't you just do them?"

"I can, but I won't. You have plenty of time on your hands, so don't be selfish. You need to be more like your mother," he replies.

It's true. I do. I have plenty of time to clean up my room and take out the trash, but I don't want to. On the other hand, Mom has no time, yet she finds a way to give it to someone else. Two summers ago, she used her vacation time to travel to third-world countries to help take water and medical advancements to those in need.

Then another time, the hospital gave her a week off, but instead of enjoying it, she volunteered at a local food pantry and was up even earlier each morning than she usually is. On the last day of that week, she spent it with me. She didn't even take time for herself. She never does. It doesn't matter how tired or burned out she is, she always makes sure everyone is doing okay. I'd give her the most selfless mom award. Or most selfless. Period.

"Okay. I'll do them," I say with a sigh.

As we pull into the school's driveway, my dad turns and looks at me. Even in the low light, I can see the bags under his eyes. Let's just say that Dad isn't used to getting up this early.

"You know the drill. Be good, don't do anything stupid, make good grades, etcetera. All that parenting stuff."

"You know you don't have to remind me," I say with my eyebrows raised.

"Yeah, I know. But I'm going to miss saying it when you leave."

"And I'll miss hearing it," I say honestly.

"Somehow, I doubt that."

"Bye, Dad."

"Have a good day, son."

I grab my bag and step out of the car, watching Dad drive away. He's working from home today, lucky him. All the lights are on inside the school, and I sigh in relief because it means it's open and I can get in. As I approach the front door, it swings open. Charlie, a scrawny redheaded freshman that is too smart for his own good, holds the door open for me. He can be annoying sometimes, but for the most part, he's cool. He has a plain white t-shirt on with some cargo shorts. He loves his plain white shirts, and I have no idea why.

"Lylon, you ready to see if our robot works?" he asks as we head down the hallway to the robotics room.

"I'm just ready to finish this project, so I don't have to come early and see you," I joke.

Charlie scowls. "Incredibly rude."

"I'm joking. Except for the part about coming early. I want to be able to sleep in again, so if we could please finish this thing, it'd be great. Also, Jen mentioned there was a problem, and it might take a while to fix it. What happened this time?" I ask.

Ever since we started this project, there have been nothing but problems. They've taken us the better part of a week to fix, but we've had very little success. Charlie deals with the robotics part while I stick to the programming. On the other hand, Jen is just with us because every other group was full. She just needed another elective, so she doesn't actually care about the class. She's not very bright and wants to be in charge of everything. She's a pain to work with, but we have no choice.

"Basically, there's a problem with the battery and the motor. I guess it's not hooked up right even though I definitely double checked when I—"

"You know what? Why don't you stick with the robotics part, and I'll stick to the programming," I say, wanting the conversation to end.

"Got it," Charlie says, taking the hint.

We walk down the hallway past all the empty classrooms, which will be full in an hour or so. The hallways are decorated for next week's homecoming. Valerie and I agree that the Friday of homecoming week is our least favorite day of the year because of all the stupid-looking mums. Some of the mums are bigger than the actual person wearing it, and it looks ridiculous. A lot of people like to put cowbells on their mums, and it's all you hear the entire day. Just thinking about it, I already want next week to be over.

Taking a left at the end of the hall and passing a few more rooms, we arrive at the robotics classroom, which is full of computers and spare parts. It looks like a bomb exploded inside a computer store. Jen is already here, so we sit down and begin working.

Over the next couple of hours, we test and retest many different methods. I triple-check my programming to confirm it is accurate, and each time it comes out okay. Finally, Charlie gets the robot properly hooked up, and it works enough to get us a passing grade. Normally, I'd try to do better than just a passing grade, but my teacher, Mr. Snyder, is a piece of work. Of course, it doesn't help that I hate the class. Programming is my strong suit, not building.

When the bell rings for second period, Charlie and I pack everything up and head out of the room. I reach my locker, and she's there. This is what I've been looking forward to all morning. Charlie stops in his tracks and stares. Valerie is at my locker waiting for me. Sometimes I get there first, and she sneaks up on me, trying to scare me, and other times I find her here waiting for me.

"That's your girlfriend?" Charlie asks without taking an eye off her.

"Yeah," I reply.

Since Charlie's a freshman and has only been here about a month, he's only heard about her but never seen her. He never believes me when I tell him how hot she is because, according to him, nerds never get the hot girls. But he's wrong, and he sees that now. Today, Valerie's hair is braided back, and she's wearing jeans with Converse sneakers and a Nirvana t-shirt. Other than mascara, she doesn't wear much make-up.

"Later, Sir Charles the Third," I say and walk toward Valerie.

"See ya," Charlie replies.

Valerie smiles at me as I approach my locker, and two perfect dimples appear on her beautiful face. Every time Valerie smiles, she brightens everything around her.

"Hey, babe," she greets me when I'm within earshot.

"Hey, beautiful," I say, my standard reply. We kiss, and her lips are soft and warm, tasting like dark roast coffee with French vanilla creamer. That's her favorite, and she drinks it every day, making me long for just a taste.

"How is the project coming?" she asks when we finish our kiss.

"Well, for now, it works, so I'm hoping for at least a passing grade."

"You're so smart. I could never figure that stuff out."

"You're also very smart, just more so when it comes to English," I reply.

"Touché," Valerie says.

I open my locker to take out my astronomy textbook before taking Valerie's hand to walk her to class.

"Hey, so I've been thinking, I know we don't want to go to homecoming, but maybe we could go out instead. Maybe grab dinner or catch a movie. Or we could have a bonfire in my backyard."

"Yeah, that sounds fun! I'd love that. I have plans to go shopping with Carly tomorrow, so maybe I'll pick out something nice to wear."

"Sweet!"

"Or you could come over to my house. My parents will still be gone so—"

"I mean we could…" I say laughing.

We continue walking until we reach Valerie's class. For second period, she has English while I have astronomy. Sadly, the only class we have together is government in the seventh period. It's got to be my favorite class, not only because Valerie is there—although that counts a lot—but because it's actually interesting.

Valerie and I stop outside her classroom.

"I'll see you later," I say.

"Can't wait," she responds with a sweet smile.

Taking her hand from mine, Valerie walks into her classroom, and I backpedal before I turn around to head to my class in the next hall over. Someone bumps into me, and I drop my textbook. I don't need to turn to know who it is. Dave is your stereotypical football jock that likes to pick on smart people, then beg for them to do his homework. I always refuse, which is why he sometimes messes with me.

Surprisingly, he never takes things too far with me, possibly because I'm number one in our class, but still, that doesn't stop him from occasionally bumping into me. Last week I walked into the bathroom and saw him forcing Charlie to drink toilet water, so I had to step in. Dave is bigger than Charlie, but he can't handle me, so he had to let Charlie go. I know I shouldn't wish for it, but I honestly wouldn't mind if Dave dropped dead.

Bending down, I pick up my book, then continue walking to my class. I'm rarely late for class, so everyone stares at me as I walk in. All of them know me for being the valedictorian, but I wouldn't call any of them a friend.

The bell rings, and Mr. Huy starts the lesson. This week we've been learning about deep space and how we might be able to achieve it. I zone out for a few minutes because Mr. Huy is really boring. I enjoy learning about space, but the guy doesn't make it interesting. All he does is stand up in front of the class and talk the whole time, most of which is his own opinion. It's a complete blow-off class, but it's still painfully boring.

I start texting Valerie, which is what we like to do when we're both bored in class. While she likes her English class, they're writing a book report, and she's already done. We text for the remainder of the second period about which *Star Wars* movie is the best. I personally think it's *A New Hope*, the original *Star Wars* movie, and she somehow thinks it's *Revenge of The Sith*. I don't know what's going through her mind right now to think that was the best *Star Wars* movie. Finally, the bell rings and I stand up, drop my phone in my backpack, and leave this wretched class.

I walk back to my locker to put my book back. It's beyond me why I bothered getting it in the first place when we never use it. I spot Valerie walking toward my locker from the opposite direction just as I start turning the rusted lock to put in the combination.

"You really think that *Revenge of The Sith* is the best *Star Wars* movie?" I ask.

"Yeah! The actor who played Anakin is kinda cute."

"Hmm."

"I mean, you are cute too," she says, tilting her head with a smile.

Just then, a crackling sounds over us, and someone starts speaking over the intercom. It's Mr. Girlin, the principal.

"Attention! All students and faculty members report to the auditorium immediately. Again, all students and faculty members report to the auditorium immediately. Thank you."

Valerie and I look at each other confused. She looks concerned, which is unlike her. I begin to grow weary myself because we've never been called down anywhere at once. Sure, we've had assemblies before, but they were always in the gym, and it was always just for students. But

Mr. Girlin called for everyone in the school. Something isn't right.

Chapter Three

10:08 AM

As if someone flipped a switch on the whole school, chaos erupts in the hallway. Some students are running, others are shouting. Valerie and I are still standing by my locker, with no clue about what's going on. I spot Anesh down the hallway. I met Anesh back in the first grade when his family moved here from India. We instantly bonded, and we've been best friends ever since. I grab Valerie's hand and hurry towards Anesh. It should only take a couple of seconds to get to him, but large groups of people are standing around, looking down at their phones. Anesh spots me and starts pushing his way through the crowded hallway toward us.

"Anesh, what on earth is going on? It was just an announcement. They're acting like the world is ending," I say as I reach him. I have to talk a lot louder than I normally would because of all the yelling.

"That's because the world might actually be ending. Pull out your phone. Mine died."

I quickly take my backpack off and dig around for my phone. When I finally find it, I press the power button, and the screen comes to life, showing a picture of Valerie and me at the beach. My hands shake from the unrest around me, and I screw up the password multiple times and almost drop the phone. When I finally get it unlocked, I notice a message and a missed call from Dad two minutes ago. My phone had been on silent, so I never heard anything. I'm instantly more worried because Dad never calls me during school hours. I hesitate for a moment before opening the text.

I'm on my way to get both you and Valerie. Stay at the school and do what they tell you. Stay safe.

Stay safe? Why wouldn't I be safe? I proceed to open my internet browser, and my heart drops into my stomach. The first news story on my timeline reads: *Alien spacecraft hovers over the capitol. Are we under attack?* Under the headline is a picture of this massive ship, the shape of a rectangle with all sorts of designs hovering over Washington D.C.

The ship looks like it's made from a black stone that resembles obsidian, but I doubt it. This ship's metal doesn't seem to be found on Earth. Massive guns are mounted on all of its sides that could easily wipe a whole city off the map. A city as big as Dallas. I turn and look at Valerie. Her eyes are wide, and she's completely frozen in shock, staring at the picture of the warship.

Only now do I notice that she's clutching my arm tightly, but I don't mind. We have bigger problems. Anesh looks like he might be sick. I've never seen him like this, not even when his dad passed away in a car accident five years ago.

So many thoughts flood my mind.

This can't be real, I keep telling myself. *That image has to be fake.*

But deep down, I know it isn't. I instantly think of my mom. She's at the hospital. Will she come home? But then maybe she'll stay and help the people that get hurt. If she has a choice, though, I know she'll stay. She always feels obligated to help whenever she can, which now might be when we need help the most.

Something touches my shoulder, and I spin around, half expecting it to be a faculty member. But it isn't.

"Lylon!" Dad yells, and he hugs me tightly to him. I can't believe he's here so fast. I just received his message.

"Dad! What's going on?!" I ask.

"I'll explain everything I can while we're in the car. You three are coming with me. That includes you, Anesh."

I'm relieved that my dad is taking Anesh with us. I'd feel bad leaving him here. He asks to borrow my phone to call his home, and I give it to him. While Anesh is talking to his mom, we try to wade through the sea of students who seem to be in full panic mode now. Some are heading toward the auditorium, and the rest – like us – head the opposite way and to the parking lot to leave.

I turn and look at my dad. "I thought you wanted us to follow directions. We're supposed to go to the auditorium."

"I wanted you to follow directions until I got here. Now that I'm here, you're coming with me, whether they like it or not," my dad replies.

We bolt towards the car and frantically throw all of our stuff in the trunk. I allow Valerie to sit up front while Anesh and I sit in the back. Dad starts the car and pulls out of the parking space. He wasn't even in all the way, evidently in a rush to get to us. Anesh finishes talking to his mom and gives my phone back.

"I called just in time. My mom was about to come to school to get me. Mr. Porter, can you please drop me off at my house?" Anesh asks.

"Of course," Dad says.

"Alright, Dad, what's going on?" I quickly ask.

"I'll tell you everything I know. Less than an hour ago, this massive spaceship of some kind entered our atmosphere and started hovering over D.C. Astronomers had no idea anything was headed our way. It's like it was cloaked somehow."

Just as Dad says this, a truck speeds past and cuts us off. Dad swerves into the next lane, the tires screeching from the sudden change of direction. We all gasp as our seatbelts lock and we start to fly forward.

"Watch it," Dad grumbles.

"I saw the picture of it when everyone went nuts in the hallway. Sorry I didn't answer your call," I say.

"Please keep the ring volume on from now on. All of you, okay?"

We all nod. Valerie hasn't said a word since she saw the picture of the ship.

"Good. Anyway, about five minutes after the first ship showed up, identical ones appeared elsewhere. Hong-Cong, Shanghai, Moscow, London, Chicago, Denver, Houston, and basically every major city of the world. There's also one in… Dallas."

As my dad says this, we round a corner, and a huge object comes into view. The ship is even more massive in person, as big as half the city of Dallas, casting a shadow over almost the entire city. My heart skips a beat, and my hands begin to sweat. Why us? There's an infinite number of planets out there, many of which are suitable for life. Why did they choose Earth?

The rest of the ride is silent. Cars are racing past us, and people stand on the side of the road watching the alien spacecraft. Valerie opens and closes her eyes as if she's trying to blink the nightmare of the ship away. Sadly for her and the rest of us, it's still here. We pull onto Anesh's street, and we spot his mom on his porch, waiting for her only son to return. I turn to him.

"Stay safe. I'll text you when I get home."

"We will. You too, man," he says and gives me a fist bump.

"Bye, Anesh," Valerie says in a small—frightened—voice. I hate hearing the sound of it. She's never this scared.

"Goodbye, Valerie," Anesh says and steps out of the car.

"Hey, Anesh," my dad calls after him.

"Yes, Mr. Porter?"

"I'm serious. Keep your phone on and stay in touch. And don't do anything stupid," my dad says.

"Okay. I'll plug it in when I get inside. Goodbye," Anesh says and turns to me. "Love ya, bro!"

I chuckle. "Love ya too."

Anesh reaches his porch, and his mom hugs him tight. She waves and mouths thank you to my dad, and he waves back. Once we start driving again, I note that lights are on in every house while people are outside in the neighborhood.

Five minutes later, we pull up to our house. I am about to ask why we didn't take Valerie home when it comes to me. Everything makes sense now. The real reason Valerie has been so quiet and sad. Her parents aren't home.

Chapter Four

10:45 AM

I've only ever lived in two houses. Even though I don't remember the house I lived in until I was three, I was told it was smaller than the house we live in now with three bedrooms and bathrooms, a living room, and a big kitchen. My parents could afford a much bigger house, but they never saw the point. The only reason we moved in the first place was because I was growing up and needed my own space.

Their philosophy is "*if we don't need it, we don't have it,*" although we do have a third bedroom we don't need. My parents always say it's the guest room, but we never have any guests to stay. None of my grandparents are alive, and my parents don't have any siblings. The only family I have is my parents. Well, and Anesh. He's definitely family. So is Valerie. I can't imagine living without her. She's there for me every day, and her smile always cheers me up no matter how I feel. I could be having the worst day of my life—like today—and she makes me feel a million times better. I need to return the favor like she did for me on her first day of freshman year.

We walk up the pathway to my house, the white brick and black wooden door greeting us. Dad fumbles with his keys until he finds the right one and opens the door. We all walk inside, and Dad locks the door behind us. For a long time, we stand in the entryway, silent, not knowing what to do. Dad stares at the floor, no doubt thinking about Mom. I'm worried about Mom, too. I can't imagine what it's like at the hospital right now. I wonder how many people have been rushed in due to car accidents or other invasion-related problems.

"Hey Dad, did you talk to Mom?" I ask, breaking the silence.

Dad sighs. "I tried her cell before I came and got you guys… she didn't pick up. But um, Valerie, I… uh, I managed to get through to your parents and they said it was fine to stay here until they get back. Actually, they prefer it. They're headed back right now, but it's a sixteen-hour drive, so it'll be a while. You can sleep in the guest room."

"Thank you, Mr. Porter. Honestly, I don't want to be alone," Valerie says, looking down at the floor.

"Travis will do. And I really don't blame you. I wouldn't want to be alone right now either." My dad pauses, nodding in understanding. "I'm going to turn on the news to see if there's anything new."

Dad leaves us alone, but I keep staring at Valerie. I want to make her feel better, but I don't know what to say.

"It's not all bad. At least your parents are together," I say the first thing that comes to mind.

Valerie's eyes are still fixed on the floor. "But both of your parents are here, and your mom is safe at the hospital."

Smooth Lylon, smooth. I should have thought better before speaking up. Valerie starts down the hallway on the left, bypassing the guest bedroom, and enters my room. I pull out my phone to touch base with Anesh, and when he texts back telling me he's fine, I go to the living room in search of Dad.

There's nothing new on TV, just images of all the different cities with warships over them. Paris shows up, an identical warship to the one over Dallas hovering over the Eiffel Tower. What are we going to do? We have to fight back, right?

"Lylon," Dad says, placing a hand on my shoulder. "I know I'm supposed to tell you everything is going to be okay, but I'm not going to. You're old enough to realize we don't have control over any of this. But I want you to know that your mother and I love you so much you can't possibly imagine. We're so proud of the young man you've become."

"I love you too, Dad," I say, and tears well in my eyes. I can't remember the last time I've cried.

Suddenly, the TV turns off, and when it turns back on a few seconds later, it's not the news but a broadcast of some kind. The image is blurry, but when it finally focuses, it reveals a hideous creature. Even from the TV, I can tell it's big and tall, with dark grey skin, pitch-black eyes, and two bottom fangs hanging over its upper lip. There are scars all over its face, and its cheekbones are sticking out way further than that of a human. Its chin is elongated, and three horns stick out of the top of its head about an inch long – or maybe more. Cold sweat runs down my spine at the sight of this hideous creature. There's no way they've come here in peace. The creature begins to speak and has a menacing deep gravelly voice.

"People of Earth. We are the Thorn, an advanced intelligent race from a planet twice the size of yours. We're not here to make peace, nor are we here to fight, but we will if we must. Our planet is dying, and we need resources. So, we're going to take everything we need, and you'll let us. If you don't cooperate, we *will* decimate you."

The image changes, showing the Thorn descending upon the Earth. Many locations all at once. They all have the same black metal armor that matches their eyes, holding giant cannons bigger than any rifle we would have. The Thorn are descending in small ships coming out of docking bays from their bigger warships. As they reach the ground, they immediately exit and start off in all directions. Hundreds of them on one transport ship, and there are hundreds of transport ships.

People are running in all directions, trampling each other, and the Thorn either shove them off or–in some instances–shoot them. The image changes to a familiar location, and I watch, horrified as these creatures march toward a hospital. East Dallas Medical Center. Dad lets out a pained sound. Valerie has quietly returned from the bedroom, because only now do I notice her as she clasps my hand, shaking her head in disbelief.

The Thorn start raiding the hospital, lining people up and aiming their cannons at them. I almost scream at the thought that they're going to execute them, but instead, they force them in the transport ships that arrived at the hospital moments ago. Are they taking prisoners? If they take them back to their own planet, they won't survive. How can they breathe outside Earth's atmosphere? And when that hideous creature talked about resources, did it mean people too? The screen changes back to the leader of the Thorn before we can see more.

"As you can see, we didn't just mean resources in the form of food, drink, and materials. In addition to our advancements in technology, we also have advanced in something else. Something that's considered a myth on your planet." The leader raises his massive hand, the size of my face, palm up. Instantly a glowing light green ball the size of a marble appears, floating above his hand. "I believe you call it sorcery on your planet. We simply call it power. One of these orbs will grant one wish, but there's a condition. The wish only works on people. If someone you care about gets killed or taken, you can wish them back. Allow me to demonstrate."

The leader takes a step back, and I blink at the sight. A man is tied to a chair and struggles to break free, grunting and begging the Thorn to let him go. His left eye is swollen shut, and there's blood and cuts on his face and arms. The leader walks to him and places his hands on the side of his head. Valerie screams at the sound of the man's neck snapping. His cries stop as his body hangs lifeless on the chair, limp.

With an evil grin in place, the leader pulls up his hand to reveal the orb again.

"I wish this man would come back to life," he growls.

The glow from the orb fades and begins to disintegrate to ash. With another crack, the man's head jerks up, and he slowly opens his eyes, frantically looking around the room. He screams again, and another Thorn grabs him, dragging him away with the chair. The screams of the man get quieter until they're no longer audible. The leader steps forward, so he's the only thing on the screen again.

"These orbs have been scattered across the world, with only one in each of the major cities we arrived at first. But where exactly is for you to find out. To what extreme will you, humans, go to save someone you love? We shall see."

The leader laughs a deep, menacing laugh as the broadcast cuts off.

Chapter Five

11:00 AM

The instant the broadcast cuts off, my dad races over to the phone. I know he'll try to reach Mom, but I fear it might be too late. My mind drifts to the last time I spoke to her, a few days ago. Usually, she works late, but she comes to say goodnight to me every chance she gets. That was one of those nights. She got home a little earlier and came straight to my room.

"Lylon? Are you awake?" she whispered.

"Yeah, Mom, I'm up," I replied slowly, already on the verge of falling asleep.

She walked over to me and sat on the edge of my bed.

"I just came to tell you that I managed to get Saturday off. Maybe we could spend the day together."

"Actually, I already have plans with Valerie," I said with a yawn.

She looked a little sad. "Okay. Maybe some other time then. Goodnight, Lylon. I love you," she said and kissed me on the forehead.

"Night, mom," I said back before drifting to sleep.

Tomorrow is Saturday, and my mom never gets Saturdays off. I feel sick. She was working so hard just to get one day off to spend it with me, and I had already made plans with Valerie. Basically, I told her I didn't have time for her. I wish things were different. I know it's not certain, but I have the gut feeling I'm never going to see her again.

I have a feeling the last image I'll have of Mom is when she sat on my bed and told me goodnight. That tired smile she gave me, then the sad look when I told her I couldn't spend time with her, and finally, the kiss on my forehead. Regret floods my mind. Regret for not spending more time with her, not thanking her enough, and not saying I love you back. And worst of all, I'll never have the chance to make things right and tell her how much she means to me.

No. I refuse to believe I'll never see her again. I simply won't accept losing her. Not her or anyone else for that matter.

"My God!" Dad says and slams the phone down.

I'm surprised at the vehemence in his voice. He doesn't get mad or upset often. Deep in thought, he pauses for a moment and takes a deep breath. I look down and notice Valerie's hand in mine. She hasn't said a word since coming into the living room. I had almost forgotten she was here. But this little contact gives me courage.

"Lylon, I… I'm so sorry," she says in a sad voice, and I nearly falter at the sight of her tearful eyes.

I want to wake up from this nightmare. Dad stays silent next to the phone as if he's waiting for the hospital to call him back. They won't. Hundreds of thoughts race through my mind, but everything seems to zero in on the way the leader brought the dead man to life.

The Thorn leader called it an orb. A wishing orb. But that's impossible. At least, he said, *we* believe it's impossible, but really, we haven't figured it out. I wonder if he's telling the truth. Why would he? He's part of an alien race that invaded our planet to take resources, and some of us prisoners, to God knows where. For all I know, it could be some hoax just to get people to kill each other for the orb.

But I won't believe that. I have to believe he told the truth, and there's a way to get my mom back. I have to get my hands on one of those orbs. The leader said that there's one in every major city they originally invaded. That means there's one here, in Dallas. I have to find it. But where do I start? There's no way Dad will let me leave the house, let alone look for it. So, I have to make a plan. Maybe I can sneak out tonight. That's good! I'll sneak out tonight while Dad is sleeping, and I'll look for the orb.

Wordlessly, I head to my room to get ready. It's a decent size room in a perfect square. My desk is at the back wall, and it's always a mess with books and papers all over. Most of it is for homework, which I'll never have to turn in. I guess that's the only good thing about this whole invasion. My laptop also sits on my desk, which I also mainly use for school.

I walk over to my closet and open the door. My closet is also a huge mess, and it's full of computer parts and remote-controlled robots from when I started attending robotics. I grab one of my backpacks and throw it on the floor. I'm about to start grabbing other things I might need when someone places a hand on my back. I spin around, expecting to find my dad, but it's Valerie.

"I'm coming with you," she says.

"W—what are you talking about?"

"I know you're going to the hospital, and I'm coming with you," she says with her hands on her hips.

"I'm not going to the hospital. I'm going to find an orb, and you're staying here."

"You really think what their leader told us is true?"

"I'm not sure, but I have to believe it. It might be the only chance to get my mom back."

"Then I'm coming with you."

"No, you're not," I say and start packing my bag.

Valerie puts her hand on my arm to stop me. "I'll either come with you, or I'll tell your dad that you're planning to leave." The serious look on her face tells me she won't back down.

"No, it's too dangerous," I say, looking her in the eye.

"Trav—" she begins, but I cover her mouth with my hand, effectively stopping her.

I feel her tongue on my palm, and I pull it away.

"Eww, you're so childish," I say, and we both burst into laughter. For a moment, we forget all about what's going on around us, and just stare into each other's eyes. I don't want her to come, not because I don't trust her, but I don't want her to get hurt or—worse—killed. But the same could happen to me. It wouldn't be fair to leave her here not knowing if I would be okay. I finally break the silence.

"Fine. You can come."

She nods and starts the preparations for our outing. I'm not sure what I should pack for an occasion such as this, but I fill my backpack with anything I can think of: a pocketknife, rope, and duct tape. We charge our phones and hide the bags under my bed so my dad won't see them if he walks in. After that, we sit on my bed, and Valerie puts her head on my shoulder.

At least half an hour goes by with us just sitting here in silence and the tumultuous thoughts in our minds. Valerie must be thinking about her parents, and I can't say I blame her. I can't stop thinking about my mom. But Valerie seems less worried now than she did when we returned from school. If she wasn't here with me, I would probably be crying again at the thought that Mom might never come back. But I need to be strong, so I won't cry in front of her.

Suddenly, a loud bang comes from the other side of the house, and we both spring up.

"Seriously?!" Dad yells.

Racing out of my room, I see Dad coming out of the pantry. I skid to a stop, and Valerie bumps into my back.

"Are you okay? What happened?" I ask my dad.

"We're out of food," he replies through his teeth.

"Like, completely?" Valerie asks.

My dad points at the pantry door, and I can see it without stepping in. All the shelves are empty. The only thing left is half a loaf of bread and a jar of peanut butter, which I know is almost empty.

"How are we out of food?" I ask.

My dad rubs his eyes. "I meant to go grocery shopping today. I had forgotten how low on food we are."

"Travis, I know this is your house, and I don't mean to add to your distress, but we can't stay here without food," Valerie says.

"Okay, okay… you're right. Ugh. Umm… I'm going to see if Brendan is home. You two check on the Bressett's. See if they have anything to spare, then hurry back," Dad says as he rushes to the front door.

Brendan is in his forties and living on his own. He divorced his wife several years ago before moving into the one-story house next door. We don't talk to him much, but I know he would help us out. The Bressett's, on the other hand, have a spoiled rotten brat for a kid and never help us out. But I guess it's worth a shot.

Valerie and I leave the house, turn right at the driveway, and cut across the yard to the Bressett's front door. All the lights are on, and their silver SUV is parked in the driveway telling us they should be home. I ring the doorbell, but when nothing happens, I start banging my fist on the door.

"Maybe they left earlier," Valerie says.

"No… no, they were here. Plus their lights are on, and car is here. I just don't get where—" I stop as something catches my attention. Through the door's side window, I can see a pool of red on the floor, reflecting the chandelier's light. Squinting, I take another look and quickly grab Valerie's arm.

"What?"

"Get back to the house."

"What, why?"

"Now!"

With no time for explanations, I clutch her arm even tighter and run to my house. As Valerie and I reach the front door of my house, my dad opens it and yanks us inside.

"Well?" he asks.

"They weren't there," I say, panting.

"Well, we don't really know that for sure," Valerie says. "Lylon freaked out, grabbed me, and ran back here."

"Their lights were on, and their car is in their driveway, but they didn't come to the door. I saw a… a pool of blood through the window."

"It could have been anything, right?" Valerie asks horrified.

"I fear Lylon is right. Brendan wasn't home either, and his lights were on, but his front door was open. I stepped inside and walked around, but it was like he vanished without a trace. His pantry was empty as well."

"He could have just left?"

"Valerie… Brendan and the Bressett's were home when we got here. I mean, why else would their vehicles be here? And we would have heard them leave," Dad says.

"Could it have been the Thorn?"

"Once again, we would have heard it. Also, why would they skip our house?"

"This makes no sense."

"Regardless, Dad, what are we going to do about food?" I ask.

Dad sighs. "There's only one thing I can think of. We need to go to the store."

"What about the Thorn?"

"There's nothing else to do, Lylon," he says, throwing his hands up. "I'll leave first thing in the morning. Who knows, maybe things will have died down a little, and it'll be somewhat safer. Perhaps I'll get the chance to go to the hospital."

"I don't like it," I say.

"Yeah, I know. But we've run out of options. We have the right to know what happened to your mother. For right now though, we need to stay as safe as possible. Keep the lights off and blinds closed and stay quiet. Make it seem like nobody is home. I'll check the news again. Maybe something has changed."

Dad heads to the living room, and I turn to Valerie.

"Are you thinking what I'm thinking?"

"That we should leave when your dad does, so we don't have to sneak out at night?"

"Exactly," I say with a small smile.

Valerie nods. "It's settled then."

I find Dad sitting on the couch watching the news and join him. There still isn't a reporter on, just live feeds from major cities. They keep showing buildings being destroyed, stores looted, people fighting, and even Thorn cutting down trees in the densely wooded areas of cities. And then I notice the top right screen.

There are two numbers.

Number of people missing/abducted: Approximately One Million.

That's too many. The Thorn have taken about a million people already, and it's only the first day they've been on Earth. And the number is only going to increase. Then I see the second number and freeze.

Number of people killed: Approximately One Hundred Million.

Dear God.

Chapter Six

5:00 PM

The news is getting worse.

Even though the number of people abducted has stayed the same, the death toll continues to rise. In the span of two hours, about fifteen million more people have been killed. In addition to the fatalities, we receive some information on the state of the world. Every military base in the world has been destroyed, and we see images and videos of bases on fire and in ruins. Clearly, the Thorn made it a top priority to ensure we can't fight back. Not that we could fight back if we wanted to. Their technology is far greater than ours, and there are too many of them. It still doesn't make any sense why they have to abduct humans.

From what the TV has shown so far, they continue to transport goods and people, with their ships flying back and forth from their warships to the surface. They're taking our metal resources, oil, precious gems, wood, and even water. I wonder how all this stuff will help them.

We're now watching the devastating images of destruction as the Thorn destroys every country's capital in the world. They've taken away our governments, something every civilization has had since the establishment of democracy. We'll have to rebuild from scratch when they leave, however many of us are left. The entire world and there's not a single form of government anywhere anymore. I never would've imagined that. But then again, I never would've imagined aliens invading Earth either.

Throughout the day, we've heard faint screams from outside, but when we look through the windows, nothing seems out of the ordinary. The screams could be coming from the next street over. I feel bad for those who are out there suffering. I can't even imagine how gruesome these deaths are. I only saw a few seconds of the Thorn shooting their cannons at people when they first started invading, but that was all I needed to see to understand how ruthless this alien race is.

I suspect they have many ways of killing, but I hope I don't find out how. What happened to our neighbors still remains a mystery, and I begin to wonder if there's anyone else left on our street. Where did they go? I feel like any second, the Thorn could bust down our door to either abduct or kill us. This fear makes me lose faith that we'll survive.

Valerie and I are sitting in the living room, the only light coming from the TV, a candle that sits on the coffee table, and what seeps through the closed blinds. We're still watching the news, hoping for some good news. Anything would do.

Dad paces around the room, scratching his chin. Even in the low light, I can see the red in his eyes. Every once in a while, he sniffles. It could be for Mom. It could be for me. Or it could be for all of us. I know he wants to keep us safe, but how can he with the Thorn running loose.

"Dad?" I ask.

"Yes Lylon?"

"Mom's smart. I'm sure she got out of the hospital. She's going to return to us. I know it."

He doesn't respond. He stares off for a while as the TV continues to play.

"Are you guys hungry?" Dad asks after a little bit, wiping his eyes.

Valerie and I nod.

"I'll go get what we have left."

We stay on the couch close to each other. Even though we aren't really watching TV, something makes me look at it. The scenery is too familiar on the screen, a tall rectangular tower with a clock on all four sides. The tower is probably thirty feet tall, with trees and benches around it. On many occasions, I met Valerie there before a date. The TV is showing the center of the park downtown. It's just another live video feed, but something catches my eye. The clock tower is damaged, and one of its clocks is missing. Half of the clock is in place on one side, but it's badly damaged with jagged edges. A faint green glow comes from inside the clock, unnoticeable unless someone paid close attention to it. The glow is the same hue of the object the leader of the Thorn had held. The glow is bound to belong to an orb!

"Valerie," I whisper, careful in case Dad is close.

"What?"

"Look at the clock tower. Do you see that glow?"

"Yeah, what about it."

"Remember what the leader of the Thorn showed us?"

Her eyes grow wide. "The orb. But it could be nothing."

"It *has* to be it," I say.

"Then we'll start there," she says, with a determined gleam in her eyes.

We sit on the couch until Dad comes back with three plates of sandwiches.

"That's the rest of our food," he grumbles.

Silently, we start eating, but I don't mind. I don't want to talk, I just want tomorrow to come as soon as possible. My mind is constantly on the mysterious orb and Mom. Is she still alive? Did they torture her? Will I see her again? I can't afford to lose hope. Not when the orb might be so near. It has to be in that clock tower. That glow was too similar for it to not be the orb.

Dad only took one bite of his sandwich before staring off into space. I know he's thinking about Mom and what to do. He places his forehead in his hand, before taking deep breaths. I just about ask him if he's alright, but before I get the chance, he gets up and swiftly exits the room. *I hope he's okay*, I think.

I glance back at the TV just as the broadcast turns off, and the screen goes all static with a whine. Valerie looks at me, confused. I try changing the channel with the remote, but the same static is on this station as well.

"Dad!" I call after him while trying to keep my voice low.

He races into the room and opens his mouth to speak but closes it when he sees the TV and realizes what's wrong.

"That's strange… Check to see if we still have internet," he says frantically.

I pull my phone out of my pocket to check if I have internet or service, but I get nothing. Great!

"I have no internet access or service on my phone," I say.

Dad sighs as he bangs his fist against the wall. "For Pete's sake!"

"What are we going to do?" Valerie asks concerned.

"I don't know! I really don't know," Dad answers as he puts his head in his hands.

A loud crash comes from outside that causes Dad to jump and Valerie to clasp her hand over her mouth. Slowly, we all turn to the front door, expecting someone or something to burst through. Dad grabs the candle off the coffee table.

"Shh, be quiet," Dad whispers.

We all pause for a moment and listen. The silence is so vast it's almost deafening. Just as I'm about to admit it was nothing, another bang reaches my ears. Dad nears the front window, and we follow him. Slowly, Dad extinguishes the candle before opening one of the curtains and we all look outside.

At first, we see nothing. It's relatively dark, and the only thing moving is the trees. When I'm about to call it quits and return to my seat, I hear an eerie scream and watch the front door of the house across the street fly off its hinges and land in the street. Two Thorn soldiers emerge, one dragging Mrs. Finnegan by her hair and the other Mr. Finnegan by his neck. Mrs. Finnegan screams for help, but she won't receive any. The Thorn soldiers throw them on the ground next to each other, and I can clearly hear Mrs. Finnegan's sobs.

Our neighbors are in their sixties and have lived in that house for nearly three decades. They used to babysit me when I was younger and even shared some holidays with us. My parents have been really close to them since we moved into this house. They're some of the nicest people we know. Certainly, they don't deserve this.

All three of us duck as the gaze of the Thorn soldier holding Mr. Finnegan sweeps past our window.

Please don't see us, please, please, please.

We stay down for a few seconds, and when we peek outside again, the Thorn look at the Finnegan's menacingly.

"I thought they were on vacation," I say, petrified.

"I thought so too," Dad says shocked.

"Can't we do something?" Valerie asks.

"I'm afraid there's nothing we can do to help them," Dad whispers.

He's right. The Thorn are even more ginormous in person. Their eight-foot-tall grey-skinned bodies tower over Mr. and Mrs. Finnegan. I don't want to watch, but I can't tear my eyes away from our friends. The Thorn soldiers take aim with their canons and pull the trigger without hesitation. The screams of Mr. and Mrs. Finnegan are heard above the gunshots. The street is dimly lit, but we can see clearly what they're doing to them. Whatever the weapon fires, it starts melting the skin right off their bodies. They scream even louder as their skin boils causing them to spasm on the ground. Steam rises into the night sky, pouring off their boiling skin.

I avert my gaze, unable to witness this brutality anymore, and dash out of the room. I run down the hall and into the hallway closet and shut the door. Falling to my knees, I clasp my hands over my ears trying to make the screams of the Finnegan's go away. All the images of the day flash in my mind, but I can't get rid of them. Why can't I make them go away?

I almost scream, but I feel a hand on my shoulder. I turn and look up to find Dad as he pulls me up into his arms.

"I can't make the screams go away," I sob.

"I can't either," he says, as he rubs my back.

"Every time I close my eyes I see the hospital, or now the Finnegan's. What do I do?"

"I don't know, I see it too… but I love you son. I love you so much. I'm going to do everything I can to make sure we get through this."

"Then stay! Don't go out there."

"I wish I didn't have to, but you know I do. We have to eat."

We remain in each other's arms for a few minutes, and when we finally pull away, Dad wipes my tears with his sleeve before wiping his own.

"I love you so much Lylon."

"I love you too Dad," I sniffle.

"Be there for her," he says, nodding in the direction of my room.

"I will," I promise and start walking toward my room.

Valerie is in my bed, with her back turned to me. Despite her sobs being barely audible, she looks so peaceful. The curves of her side are visible, and her beautiful hair flows onto the pillow. I take off my shoes and shirt before climbing into bed next to her. She immediately turns around and puts her head on my chest as I close her into my arms. We stay silent for a moment, but I'm tired of silence. I need to hear her voice.

"Who are we if we can't protect the ones we love?" I ask.

Valerie thinks for a while. "We're only human. That's all we ever are." There's another moment of silence before Valerie speaks up again. "We'll get through this."

"How do you know?"

"I don't." She sniffles. "Maybe it's intuition, or I wish for it so bad, it's the only outcome I want. Either way, I refuse to give up as long as you're by my side."

I want to say more, but I can't argue with that. I grab my phone from the nightstand, but there's still no service. We really are on our own. If Valerie really believes we'll be all right, then I choose to believe it as well.

Right now, though, I need to get some sleep. Tomorrow's a big day. The day I make things right. The day I find an orb and get my mom back.

Chapter Seven

Day Two

Last night I dreamt of Mom. A nightmare. I dreamt she was being tortured and forced to do unimaginable things for the Thorn. I tried to save her, but my legs were jelly. I tried to scream, but my voice didn't carry. I woke up at 7 a.m. sweating. I can't get her out of my head, even when I'm sleeping. The guilt, the sadness, all those emotions that have built up inside me are getting too much for me to handle.

But today, everything changes.

Today, we get her back. Faint light slips through my window, but it's enough to know it's close to seven. The clock on the nightstand reads 6:58 a.m. Dad will be leaving soon, which means we'll have to get ready to leave as well.

I forgot that Valerie was here, even though it's the first time a girl slept in my bed. Her arm is on my chest, still in the same position she was when she fell asleep. When I was younger, I used to toss and turn a lot in my sleep. Often times I would wake up on the floor, or my feet would be at my pillow. When I got older, that changed. I don't move around much anymore, which is good since it means I let her sleep in peace.

I'm glad tiredness took over my racing mind. With everything that happened and the nightmare, I didn't get a good night's sleep. But seeing Valerie next to me when I opened my eyes brought a smile to my face. She slides her hand up to her face and takes a deep breath as her eyes slowly open.

"Good morning, beautiful," I say and stroke her hair.

"Morning," she says with a smile and kisses me.

"I didn't wake you, did I?"

"No. What time is it?"

"Seven o'clock. We'll need to get going soon," I say with a faint smile.

"Okay."

Valerie gets up and puts her jeans on. I try not to look, but she catches me and smiles. I wish I could just lay here with her forever, but we can't. We have work to do. Getting out of bed, I walk over to the window and look outside. It's a foggy morning, and I can only see a few yards into the yard that separates my house from the street.

Closing the curtain, I walk over to the wardrobe and throw on a sweatshirt and change into jeans. Since it's a cool morning, I give Valerie one of my jackets and exit the bedroom. Dad is nowhere to be found. Going to the kitchen, I find a note on the counter in Dad's handwriting.

Went to the store. Stay at home with the doors locked.

Love,

Dad.

So, he already left without telling me goodbye. I hope last night wasn't the last time I will ever see him. I try not to think about him not returning, but I can't help myself.

"He already left," I tell Valerie.

"I guess we have to get going then."

I nod. "Yeah, I guess so."

"There's been a change of plans," she says.

"What are you talking about?"

"We are splitting up. I am not going with you."

I raise my eyebrows. "What do you mean we're splitting up?"

"You're going to find the orb, and I'm going home. You already know where the orb is, so you don't need my help to find it. And you're perfectly capable of getting it yourself. I am going to see if my parents have returned or if they tried to call. Plus, we might have some supplies there in case your dad returns empty-handed."

"I don't like it," I say after a long pause. "I hate the idea of not being together when the world is going down the drain."

"I don't like it either, but we need to. Plus, we might slow each other down. You need to find that orb, and I need to get to my house. If we are careful, we should be fine."

Should be fine. That's what I don't like. Many things could go wrong, and we don't have a way to communicate. But I have to respect her need to know if her parents are okay.

"Fine, but promise me at the first sign of trouble, you run, and you don't stop until you get here."

"I promise. We'll be okay. I just know it," she says.

I head back into the living room and turn on the TV. Every channel is still static, so we have no update on anything. I don't think we'll get the TV or internet back. The only things they showed us anyway were depressing numbers and horrible videos. Expectedly, the only updates we'll be having from now on will be about the increasing death toll. I turn off the TV.

It's time to head out.

Valerie and I grab our bags and leave the house. Across the street are two skeletons, and images of last night's events flash through my mind. The Finnegan's were forced out of their home and executed prisoner style in their own yard. The images of their skin boiling off their bodies keep flickering in my mind. Tears well up, but I quickly wipe them away.

Nothing makes sense. What determines who gets killed? Why did they select the Finnegan's? I thought they just wanted our resources. That's what the leader of the Thorn said. Maybe that's what he intended, but his soldiers are taking it too far. I doubt the leader cares, but it makes no sense why they randomly selected a house on my street.

In order to avoid seeing the Finnegan's remains up close, Valerie and I walk a few houses down before crossing the street. We stay between houses to avoid being seen, but the neighborhood seems deserted. It's very quiet with a slight breeze and the occasional bird chirping. Where is everyone? I know Dad said that many people had packed up and left, but he couldn't have meant the whole neighborhood. There should still be some people hiding in their houses, but it doesn't seem like it.

Once we make it a few streets down, we stop and look at each other. This is where we split up. I'll have to turn right for the downtown park, and Valerie left for her house. I tuck a strand of hair behind Valerie's ear and kiss her. Her lips are cold, but I don't care. This might be the last time we kiss. I try not to think about that, but the thought is there. We kiss for a while, and I don't want it to end. I finally pull away, knowing our time is up. The longer we stay in the streets, the more we run the risk of being discovered.

"I love you," I say.

"I love you too."

This is the first time we ever said it to each other.

Chapter Eight

Travis

While Lylon and Valerie were sleeping, I packed my bag and got ready to leave. And by packing, I mean grabbing an empty backpack to get as much food as possible from the store, and a pocketknife for protection.

All night, I couldn't sleep, keeping watch in case someone entered our house. Every five minutes, I changed rooms to have a view from every part of the house. It was quiet, and there was no suspicious activity the entire night, but I still didn't allow myself to sleep. I had to keep vigil and be ready to wake up Lylon and Valerie at any moment if something didn't seem right. What would we do? Probably run, but it never came to that.

As soon as Lylon went back to his room last night, I wept. I know I need to give him hope that we'll make it, but as soon as he left, I couldn't hold back any longer. I wept for the Finnegan's unjustified gruesome death. I wept for the world because no matter how evil humanity can be, we don't deserve this.

I wept for my wife. Liza is the love of my life, and no matter how many years have passed, she still takes my breath away. Her smile, her kindness, the way she cares about everyone fascinates me. I can't accept that she was killed or abducted. Either way she was taken from us!

I also wept for Lylon because I might lose him for good. He might not get to experience the world in full, graduate high school, go to college, travel the world, or have his own family.

Just before I left, I went to my son's room. Sure enough, he and Valerie were fast asleep. The sight of their peaceful sleeping bodies brought a smile to my face.

I wanted to tell Lylon I was leaving, but I didn't want to wake him or Valerie. I was happy they were able to get some sleep despite everything going on. Or perhaps I didn't want to say goodbye. I didn't want Lylon to think I may not make it back. Whatever happens, nothing will stop me from returning to my son.

It's around 6:30 when I leave the house. It's mostly dark out. There's a slight breeze, and it's getting foggy. Thankfully, the closest store, Glenn's, is only a mile away, right before you turn into our neighborhood. I cut between houses to stay out of sight. I'm heading down the alley that will lead me to the back of Glenn's when I hear a jingle from behind. Shivers run down my spine, and I stop in my tracks, worried I'm about to get jumped.

"I—I don't want any trouble," I say, raising my hands in the air. "I just need to get some food for my family, that's all."

My rampant heart continues to accelerate as the jingle gets closer. There's a click with each step the being takes. Closer and closer. I can feel it right on top of me, and I realize it's too late to run. I start to accept my fate when a cold, wet tongue licks my exposed left ankle. Surprised, I look down and find a small German Shepherd licking my leg.

"Geeze, dog. You scared the crap out of me," I say and look around to make sure there's nobody else.

I bend down to pet the dog, and as it begins to lick my face, I nearly gag at the smell of his wretched breath.

"Okay, okay, that's enough," I say with a smile.

My glasses fog up from his breath, and I have to wipe them down before examining the dog's jingly collar. The shiny metal of the bell creates a shimmer despite the fog surrounding us, and I see the name Rudy engraved into the top. The only thing the bell says is Rudy, with no home address to return him.

"So, your name's Rudy?" As soon as he hears his name, Rudy's ears shoot up, and he starts wagging his tail vigorously. "Alright, Rudy. You hungry? Let's go get some food."

I continue down the alley with Rudy right by my side. His head, ears, and tail remain up, so I assume he's happy to be around another human again. I wonder what happened to his owners and how long he's been on his own.

We reach the end of the alley, and I climb over a short chain-link fence to get to the back of Glenn's. Thankfully, there's a hole in the fence a little further down, which Rudy instantly spots and slips through. He trots over to me with his tail still wagging and his tongue hanging out. When we reach the steps to lead us to the store, I stop for a moment to listen. Not even crickets chirp.

Slowly, I open the already cracked door and step inside with Rudy. My shoulders slump, and I sigh at the sight before me. There's no doubt I'll fill up my backpack but navigating the store will take a while. Items are everywhere, racks are overturned, and the ceiling is down in one of the aisles. It looks like a tornado blew through the store. I turn on the flashlight on my phone to navigate through the dark store.

I start up and down the aisles and take anything I can find. Chips, bread, bottled water, basically anything we can eat without cooking. The good thing about my wife being a nurse is that we're constantly stocked up on medicine, so we're good on that. There are other good things too, but time is not one of them. I miss seeing my wife every night at dinner or telling her to have a good day in the morning. And I know Lylon misses spending time with her despite not admitting it. I pray she's at the hospital when I arrive.

I finish filling the backpack with food, I even manage to find a chocolate bar. I head to the pet aisle, probably the only aisle that's completely stocked. I guess pet owners didn't think about feeding their pets. I grab a bag of treats and stick it in the side pocket of the backpack, and then I grab the smallest bag of dog food there is and open it. Rudy devours half the bag, and I barely manage to squeeze the rest of the dog food into the backpack. I know it won't last long, but it'll have to do for now. I wonder how Lylon will react to me coming home with a dog. My son always wanted a dog, and I'm honestly surprised that we haven't gotten one already, but he'll get one now.

"Alright, Rudy. Time to get my wife," I say, and we head out of the store, toward the hospital a few blocks away.

Chapter Nine

Lylon

Immediately after splitting up with Valerie, I realize it's a mistake. Sure, I want to find the orb, and she wants to get to her house, but we shouldn't be on our own with everything going on. Am I being selfish for wanting the orb for myself? For all I know, Valerie could need the orb just as much. Does that make me selfish if I don't let her or anyone else use it? But it can only be used once. The leader of the Thorn wondered to what lengths we were ready to go to get our hands on one. Has anyone else used an orb? How many people have died trying?

I continue to weave in-between houses to stay out of sight. Every once in a while, I hear a gunshot in the distance, and it scares me every time. It's weird the only bodies I've seen so far are the Finnegan's, considering the last update we had was over a hundred and fifteen million deaths. With thousands dying every second, how is it that I've only seen two bodies? Don't get me wrong, I'm glad I haven't seen more bodies, but you would think there would be a lot more, considering the city feels deserted. I've only seen two Thorn in person, which is also weird since I saw several hundreds of them descending from their warships. Am I the only one questioning what's happening?

I pass some houses with broken windows and holes in the brickwork. Bullet casings are strewn all over the street, next to dried blood, and to my horror, I realize there was a shootout here. Hopefully whoever was involved isn't here anymore because I don't want to get shot. The park is ahead. All I have to do is cross the street, but I can't. At least not yet. Five Thorn soldiers are pacing back and forth in the park, just under the clock tower. It's a good sign because it tells me there must be an orb there. On the downside, it might also mean they can take or kill me. I crouch behind a tree and wait, watching them from afar like a sniper, clocking his surroundings. Five minutes pass, then ten, and they're still there. Are they ever going to leave?

Suddenly, one of them starts to walk out of the park, and the others follow. But as they do so, the soldier at the front fades until he vanishes into the wind. He was there a second ago, but now he's gone. I feel stupid. How did I not think of this before? Why we haven't seen so many of them. They've been cloaking themselves. They did it with their spacecraft, and that's how they reached Earth undetected.

I should've known they can cloak themselves as well. For all I know, there could be one spying on me right now, and that makes going outside even more dangerous than we thought. That still doesn't explain not seeing any corpses. Once again, nothing makes sense.

I give it another five minutes to make sure another one doesn't show up. If I'm being watched, I need to get somewhere safe, like back home. But since I'm already here, I might as well go ahead with my plan. Speed is of the essence, so I bolt across the street, keeping my body low.

The park is peaceful. Despite it being October, the grass is still green, and the leaves are colored. The peaceful scenery brings a smile to my face, and I feel happy, almost forgetting my mission. This is my favorite time of the year because it's idyllic walking through the park. Usually, kids are running, riding their bikes, skating, playing, yelling, and screaming. Moms and dads out with their toddlers and people walking their dogs. But my smile quickly fades as I remember what's happening to the world. The park is vacant and will be for a long time—maybe forever.

I take the concrete pathway leading to the clock tower, hoping that the orb is there and that if it is there, it hasn't already been taken. Hoping that a Thorn soldier won't attack me as I'm trying to get it. Up until now, I've been confident that it will be there, but I'm starting to have my doubts. Perhaps I wanted the orb to be there and I imagined the whole thing. I guess I'm about to find out.

I finally make it to the clock tower and try the wooden door. I grab the knob, and it squeals as I rotate it as far as it will go. I pull the door as hard as I can, but it doesn't budge. It's locked, and I realize I have to find another way in. I walk around the clock tower in search of another door even though I already know there isn't one. Glass crunches under my foot when I round the back of the tower, reminding me of the broken clock I saw on TV. I gaze up at the clock, which is half-broken with the other half hanging down, creating a big gaping hole, and wonder if I can get in through there. It would be a thirty-foot climb with nothing to hold on to. The clock tower is made of a smooth brick that I would probably slide down if I tried to climb it. But not if I had something to help me climb.

The rope and duct tape I packed last night comes to mind, and I take them from my backpack. I knew they'd come in handy. Maybe I can get the rope through the hole where half of the clock used to be and scale the wall. It's worth a shot, but first, I have to find something to get the rope up there. I look around for anything I can use, and I find a stone roughly the size of my fist. It's big enough for me to tie the rope to but small enough to get wedged into something.

I tie the rope around the four sides of the stone and securely wrap the whole stone in duct tape, just to make sure it'll hold. When I finish, I take a few steps back, ready to throw the stone up at the tower. I've never been good at sports, so I doubt I'll make it on the first try, but I won't stop until I get in that tower, one way or another.

Bringing my hand behind my head, I throw the stone as hard as I can. It flies toward the tower fast but bounces off the brick a few feet below the broken clock and falls back down. I have to jump out of the way to avoid getting hit by my own throw as the rock connects to the concrete a few feet in front of me. I pick the rock back up to throw again, this time aiming higher. Instead of flying smoothly through the opening, it crashes through the remaining piece of the broken clock, and I shield my eyes as glass shards fall in every direction. Bits and pieces land in my hair, and I shake my head to get them out. So much for being quiet.

I stroll up to the tower wall and grip the rope with both my hands. Back in freshman gym class, I used to climb ropes, and I wasn't too bad at it, but that was years ago. Leaning back, I tug the rope and hear something crackling from above. It holds. I guess the rock has caught onto something. Smiling, I start climbing, but I'm not more than four feet up when the rock gives way and I find myself falling backward, landing on my back. The rock cracks against the concrete a few feet from my head and splits into two.

"Wow… That didn't work," I whisper.

I dust myself off as well as I can and pick up one of the two pieces of the rock, peeling the duct tape off. That's when it comes to me! I rush to the door again and look at the doorknob. This won't be quiet, but I'm running out of options.

BANG! BANG! BANG!

Third time's the charm, and the doorknob rolls around on the ground. I squeeze four fingers into the hole and pull as hard as I can.

Success.

"Straight out of a movie," I mumble.

The inside of the clock tower is cold and damp, with gears and spiderwebs everywhere. All four clocks are accessible through the center ladder that leads to the platform on the top. My shoes crunch from the broken glass as I climb the ladder. The gears are slowly rotating with a clank with every full rotation. The ladder is completely open, so the whole thirty-foot ascent will be a long and dangerous one, but I have no other choice. It's still safer than using the rope to climb the outside wall of the clock tower. When I'm about ten feet up, I see the faint light-green glow. The higher I climb, the brighter the orb gets.

By the time I reach the top, my arms and legs are burning. I wonder how often someone needs to climb this ladder for maintenance. As soon as my head pokes above the platform, my heart drops into my stomach. A solar-powered lamp sits in the center of the platform and shines in all directions to illuminate the four clocks at night. It's been tipped over, though, so one side shines up, giving the whole space a glow.

"I'm so stupid!" I mumble and pull my body up and rest on the platform.

How could I have thought that was the orb? Maybe the colors were off on TV, giving it that green glow, but it's clearly a light yellow, and I should have known better since I've seen the clock tower at night before. Frustrated, I pick the lantern up and throw it off the ledge. It hits the wall before smashing on the ground with a loud bang, making me feel even more stupid for making so much noise.

I look over the edge of the platform to find the lantern smashed into several pieces. Four bulbs are broken on the ground while the casing rests a few pieces away. Then I spot another circular object with a flashing light in its center. Something about it isn't right. The black metal doesn't seem to belong in a cheap lantern.

It looks alien.

Curiosity gets the better of me, and I hurry down the ladder. The small saucer-shaped object that's no bigger than my hand rests at my feet, so I pick it up. I'm surprised by the heavy weight of it. Some symbols are etched on top, but they're unlike anything I've ever seen before. The flashing light in the center seems to be a button. Without thinking, I push it in the whole way, and suddenly find I'm no longer in the clock tower.

Chapter Ten

Valerie

I didn't want to separate from Lylon, but it was necessary. Yes, I want to help him find the orb, but at the same time, I don't want to be with him when he does. I'm sure he'll find it because that glow on TV was too obvious, but I have a strange feeling about it. What if I need the orb too? I have no idea what has happened to my parents or if they're still alive. If they're dead, then I need the orb as much as Lylon. But I don't want to take it from him. The Thorn want humanity to fight for the orbs, but I don't like that. I don't want to fight anyone. Nobody deserves what has happened, but we shouldn't be tempted with powers we don't understand. So, I want to pull myself from the running. Sure, I'll root for Lylon from the sideline, but I take no part in this stupid war. I refuse to lose my own humanity because of greed.

I'm a couple of blocks away from my house. When my family first moved here, I cried for days because I didn't want to leave the beautiful mountains of Colorado. The first week we came here, I kept saying that I wanted to move back. But then, things changed. On my first day of school, I met Lylon. I'm usually very popular, able to make friends quickly because of my looks, but these friendships never last for long. At my previous school, though, I had a lot of real friends. But then, when I transitioned to high school, my dad got a good job offer, and we moved to Dallas a few weeks later.

On the first day at my new school, I was getting my schedule when the counselor asked a boy to show me around. From the first time I saw Lylon, I felt a pull to him. His cute smile complemented his square jaw, and I was locked to his soft brown eyes, as he ran his fingers through his dark hair. He always tells people he didn't think anything of meeting me that day and that he was perfectly calm, but we both know it's a complete lie.

He tried to speak, but he lost his train of thought more than once and had to start over, while his hands were shaking like a leaf in the wind. I thought it was cute. He tried to act nonchalant, but he failed, and I could tell he was into me. But I was acting the same way. Sure, I was nervous being at a new school, but mostly because of Lylon. When I started talking to him more, I was thrilled that we had so much in common. And when he asked me out a week later, I was over the moon.

At the time, my parents weren't too fond of me dating Lylon, but that changed after they finally met him. And when they met his mom at an open house at the school, they were very impressed. Then I finally got the full approval to date Lylon.

After I met him, I promised myself I wouldn't let this school be like the rest. I wouldn't let my looks decide who my friends were, refusing to turn into a snob like some of the other pretty girls. It was the best decision I made in my life. My grades improved, and now I'm—or was—top ten in our senior class. Of course, Lylon is number one, but he doesn't brag. It's not his style.

But he is an explorer, or at least wants to be one. Part of me wishes we had run away together months ago, to live the best life has to offer and explore new places. I wish we had been in the middle of nowhere, on some mountain or in some valley when the Thorn entered the atmosphere. Then it would have been just us, and we wouldn't have to worry about being taken or killed in our sleep. Then again, things might have been harder this way because we'd constantly worry about our families. At least Lylon is with his dad. I need to find out what happened to my parents.

Moving quickly between houses, like Lylon told me, I round another corner. My house is only a street away. The fog has started to clear, but it's a little hazy. The neighborhood seems deserted, just like Lylon's, the only sounds coming from the occasional chirping of a bird or leaves rustling. I'm so used to hearing cars or motorcycles, it feels like I am inside of a vacuum chamber. But I'm not. This is the apocalypse.

I cut through one more alley before making it to my street. The moment I see my house in the distance, I realize something is off. The front door is open, and one of the windows is shattered. On top of that, my parent's car is nowhere to be seen. They can't be home. Or if they are, they must be hurt, or worse.

"Mom? Dad?" I call out when I get to the porch.

There is no answer. The door creaks as I push it wide open. My heart is racing and adrenaline pumps through my veins. I feel like something will pop out at any second, just like a horror movie. But this is my home, not a movie. Holding my breath, I inch farther into the house, the wooden boards creaking under my shoes. I can't stay here long.

I head straight to my parents' room and find it empty, so I race to my room and lock the door behind me in case someone is here or around the house. As I pack my bag, I notice that some of my outfits are missing. Honestly, I don't mind. Perhaps the person who took them needed them more.

I take the rope out of my bag since it's wasted space and wonder if Lylon has used his rope yet, or if he is going to. I'm worried if he's okay. I wonder if he's found the orb and if he has gotten his mom back. I wonder what it's like to use an orb or what it's like to come back from one. Actually, I hope I won't have to find out.

The last item I put in my bag is a picture of my parents and me on our trip to Canada. We went when I was a sophomore, and it was the first time I traveled out of the country. It was beautiful there and was the best vacation ever. I only wish Lylon had come with us. I had wanted to invite him, but it was my family's yearly getaway. Those vacations have always been just me and my parents.

I give my room one last look. The teal walls and birchwood furniture have so many memories. In all probability, I'll never return to this room, and it breaks my heart to think about it. While it wasn't my first room, and I hated it at first, it soon became my favorite. This is where Lylon and I shared our first kiss, a memory I'll cherish forever.

Slowly, I creep out of my room. It's unsettling to think that someone broke into our house and didn't take any electronics or money, just clothes, medicine and probably food. That's just the world we live in. Who knows when or if the Thorn will return to their planet. I fear they'll stay here and finish us off. I can only pray they won't.

I make it to the kitchen, and sure enough, the pantry is empty. I walk over to the counter where the phone is. I honestly don't know why we still have a home phone. Mom and I constantly tell Dad it's unnecessary because nobody calls anymore, and we all have our cellphones. But

Dad is adamant, insisting on keeping it for emergencies. I wonder now if Dad was right.

The machine blinks with two new voicemails, and I quickly pick up the phone to listen to the messages.

"Va—Valerie, if you're listening to this, call us back as soon as you can," Dad says in an urgent—almost panicky—voice. "I tried calling your cell, but you didn't pick up. We're on our way home, but it'll be a while. If you can, stay at a friend's, preferably Lylon's. His parents will know what to do."

There's a long pause, and then Mom's voice echoes through the phone. "Hey, sweetie! Whatever you do, stay inside and don't answer the door. Be smart and stay safe. We'll be home as soon as possible. We love you so much. Goodbye, sweetheart."

The voicemail ends with a click as my heart sinks into my stomach. They were on their way home. But where are they now? The second voicemail instantly begins playing.

"Hello Ray family residence. My name is Sheriff Richard Pines of Pueblo, Colorado. If I have this right, then I should be speaking to Valerie Ray. I called to let you know that your parents have been involved in a serious accident. I know there's an invasion going on, but you have the right to know. Your parents didn't make it. I'm truly sorry, and I hope you are doing okay. Call me back if you get the chance. Stay safe."

I stare at the phone in disbelief, then drop it as my heart bursts into a million little pieces.

Chapter Eleven

Travis

Rudy and I leave the store, but I can't stop thinking about Lylon and Valerie. I need to get home as soon as possible, yet I'm heading in the complete opposite direction. I'm really banking on everything being okay when I return. I worry in case someone tries to break into our house, or a Thorn soldier attempts to take them. But at this point, I can only dream all will be okay.

If something happens while I'm gone, I'll never forgive myself. It's my responsibility to keep them safe, and instead of staying with them, I'm heading out into a warzone to find out if my wife is okay. Granted, we need food, but I already have that. I could go home right now, and we'll be okay, but I want to see if Liza is still here. Does this make me selfish?

Lylon and Valerie are very smart, and if something happened, they'd react fast. They would probably run to a safe place, but then I wouldn't have a way to find them when I got back. Once again, I pray that I'll return to find them fast asleep.

The hospital is now only a block away. The streets are deserted, with wrecked cars and people's belongings strewn everywhere. It looks like a ghost town. All these corporate buildings with thousands of offices seem empty when usually, you can't walk down the street from all the people rushing about. I wonder where all those people went. Chances are that not all of them survived, but they couldn't have all vanished either.

I pass a barbershop with all of its windows blown out and a completely trashed cellphone repair shop. I wonder who was in their right mind to go tagging in the middle of an invasion. I didn't even want to go out to get food, but I had to.

The hospital comes into view, and I look at the eight-story tan brick building. It's a very big hospital with over a thousand rooms. The neon hospital sign on the top is flickering with the P completely out. Windows are broken, and two ambulances out front are upturned. I hate the sight. After everything, I can't stand to see the place broken.

Carefully, I reach the hospital front doors and grab Rudy's collar so that he doesn't run into the place. I can tell he's eager to sniff around and explore because his tail is wagging faster than when he first saw me. Glass shards are all over the ground from where the front door has shattered, so I climb through the frame and guide Rudy through to make sure he doesn't step on any glass. He's a very smart dog. He seems to already know how to avoid the glass. The inside of the hospital gives me the creeps. Lights are flickering, illuminating the empty and devastated space. The hallways have overturned beds, papers, and machines everywhere. It's eerily quiet, the only noise coming from the buzzing lights.

"Hello? Anyone here?" I call out.

"Who are you, and what do you want?" a woman yells, coming from the hall behind me.

My heart skips a beat when the woman comes closer and raises her hand to point a gun at me. Rudy growls and she points the gun at him. She's a short woman around thirty dressed in a nurse's uniform, with her brunette hair pulled back into a bun. Her eyes are red like she's been crying.

"Whoa, easy. Lower the gun. We're not here to hurt you," my shaky voice says.

"That's what those creatures told us, but they lied."

Rudy growls louder this time, and I lean down to pat his head. "Rudy, easy."

Rudy seems to relax as he stops growling and sits down. I turn my attention to the woman once more. She's shaking, and the gun moves up and down, making me nervous that at any time, something might set her off.

"Please, lower the gun so we can talk. Human to human. Okay?" She hesitates for a moment, but then she lets out a resigned sigh and lowers the gun as if it doesn't matter. I guess at this point, it doesn't.

"If you want meds, just get them and go," she says.

"I don't need meds. What happened here?" I ask.

For a moment, she just stares at me and then begins to sob. Slowly, I walk over to her, and she drops the gun, falling into my arms. I lead her to one of the beds, and we sit down.

"Th—th—they," she starts, but the ugly sobs racking her whole body don't let her continue.

"Shh. It's okay. You're okay." I realize I'm comforting her like I would Liza, but she needs it. I let her cry some more, passing her a tissue from one of the bedside tables.

"What's your name?" I ask a while later when she calms down.

"Janice," she responds with a sniffle.

"It's nice to meet you, Janice. My name is Travis Porter. Can you tell me what happened here?" I expect her to start crying again, but instead, she stays silent for a moment, wipes her eyes, and takes a deep breath.

"We were working. Incidents kept coming in for car accidents, gunshot wounds, anything and everything.

People were freaking out from the warship hovering over the city. That's when they descended on us." Janice pauses for a moment to wipe her nose. "As soon as we saw them outside, I hid under the counter. People were getting taken and shot. They had these weird cannons, and when they shot them, people's skin would fall right off. I stayed under the counter, but it didn't matter. They found me, and I thought it would be the end. Instead, they told me that I'm the last one here and I must stay here. They said they'll kill me if I leave."

"What about the patients?" I ask.

She looks at me with wide eyes, and I can tell the answer isn't good. "They killed them all."

I wince at the thought of sick and injured people executed in their hospital beds. I'm disgusted. It went from just taking resources to abducting humans and killing innocent people for no reason. What will they do next?

"I'm so sorry. I can't even imagine what you went through. But they aren't around. I didn't see them anywhere. I think you can leave."

"No, you don't understand. They can be anywhere. They can cloak themselves and turn invisible," Janice says with a sad look. "I can't leave."

I hadn't thought of that. Self-cloaking devices. Of course. That would explain not seeing them outside much. But that means they could've been following me the whole time. And if I'm being watched, I can lead them straight to home. They can be anywhere, and we won't know it. I decide I'm done waiting. I need to hurry.

"My wife. She uh… she works here. Well, I guess she used to. Her name is Liza Porter."

"Your wife is Liza?"

"Yeah. You know her?" I can't bring myself to ask if she's dead.

"That explains why your name is familiar. I knew Liza. We often worked together. All she would ever talk about was your son, Lylon. She was an incredible person, never missing a shift, always running to everyone's aid. She's an angel. She's not dead if that's what you're asking."

"Then… where is she?" She looks at the floor, and my fears are confirmed without Janice answering my question.

"I'm so sorry, Travis. They took her. And they put her on a transport ship… She's not coming back," Janice says with a tone of finality in her voice.

Slowly I nod and stand up. Rudy follows me as I walk to the front door. Just before I leave, I turn back to Janice.

"I'm sorry you have to be here. Stay safe." I don't wait for a response. I walk out of the hospital and start towards home. Lylon and Valerie are my number one priority. I never should have left them. The air is starting to warm up, and my watch reads ten o'clock. I can't believe I've been gone that long.

I walk back to the street from where I came, with the wrecked cars, the barbershop with smashed windows, and the vandalized phone repair shop. Mentally, I had prepared myself for the news that Liza would be gone for good, but now my heart is breaking into a million pieces. But I don't cry. I'm done crying about this. I cried all night believing that Liza was taken, and now that my greatest fears are confirmed, all I feel is emptiness.

How will I break the news to Lylon? I think that he still hopes his mom will come back. I do too, but after seeing the broadcast and what the Thorn are doing, I have lost hope. And now, after finding out for sure she was taken, I don't believe my beautiful Liza will survive or ever return to us.

It's hard to appear optimistic around Lylon. I know I need to, but it isn't easy. That's why I told my son that I couldn't tell him everything would be okay. Parents are supposed to make their children feel safe, but I can't lie to him about this. He's old enough to figure it out for himself.

I make it back to the store I was at about an hour ago, and I decide to go back in to get off the streets. Rudy is still following alongside me, watching everything like my bodyguard. I wonder if he wants to protect me. I also wonder what he would do if he saw a Thorn soldier. Would he attack him or just bark? He clearly knows what a gun is, so he's had training of some kind, but I doubt he's ever had to deal with hostile aliens.

Nobody was prepared for this.

Rudy and I leave from the back of the store, and I jump over the fence while Rudy goes through the hole. We walk down the alley, exit onto the street, and immediately cross over to stay out of sight. We weave between houses and cut through some streets until we're a street away from home. When it comes into view, I'm relieved that it's still standing in one piece. It looks exactly like it did when I left. There aren't any broken windows, and the front black wooden door is closed.

I race down the street with Rudy in tow. The last time I ran with a dog, I was a kid. I had a dog named Max that I took everywhere with me. Good memories. I hope Lylon has time to create his own happy memories.

Carefully, I near the door and quickly unlock it. Rudy is facing the street as I unlock the door, still watching for any signs of trouble. He's going to be a great dog to have around. The dog races past me inside and begins to sniff everything while I lock the door behind me. I'm worried someone followed me or saw me entering, but I put the thought to the back of my mind.

"Lylon? Valerie? Are y'all up?" I call but get no answer.

Immediately, I rush to Lylon's room and find it empty. If his room is empty, they're awake, and if they're awake, they should've answered me. My heart beats faster as I check every room in the house. Where are they? It isn't until I reach the kitchen that I get the answer. On the counter, I find a sticky note that wasn't there this morning.

Dad, if you're reading this, Valerie and I are looking for an orb to get Mom back. Checking the park first.

Love, Lylon

It all makes sense now. The reason Lylon was so optimistic believing his mom will return. He's been planning to look for the orb all along.

Chapter Twelve

Lylon

I stand in a room lit only by strips embedded in the walls. The walls are made of some kind of black metal, resembling the Thorn warship and the device I was just holding. How am I here? One moment I'm in the bottom of the clock tower, and the next, here. In the blink of an eye, I teleported here. Where even is here? Could I be on a Thorn ship? Is this possible? But then again, how are the orbs possible?

There's only one big metal door on the opposite wall with a window in the center. Tentatively, I peek and find another massive room in a perfect square. The ceiling has to be at least thirty feet high. In the center of the room, a glowing object the size of a marble is floating. The orb.

"No way!" I say with an ear-to-ear grin.

I'm happy to see the orb, but there's something else in there. Flying around the orb is a column of air that looks like a tornado. It swirls around the room, defending the orb. But what is it defending the orb from?

For a moment, everything clears, and I see four people. One is in the far back corner, motionless, while two guys push at each other on the left wall. The last guy is on the right, trying to jump for the orb but getting thrown back into the wall by the wind. How did they all get here?

I continue to watch them struggle as I ponder what to do. I no longer have the device, so teleporting back isn't an option. If I join, it will be a challenge, but I'm here, and there's nothing else I can do.

I place my hand on the door, and it swings open. The wind immediately sucks me into the room. I try to grab ahold of the doorframe but am unsuccessful and go flailing through the air. I pass right by the orb and reach my hand out, but it passes through my fingers. I slam into the far wall knee first and I yelp from the pain.

"Come on, Lylon, you didn't think it'd be that easy, did ya?" a voice calls to my left.

I turn and find Brett, a kid from my astronomy class, his eyes heavy. His leg is twisted behind him at an unnatural angle, and I can tell it's broken.

"Jeez, Brett, what happened to you?" I ask. The wind howls so loud I have to yell.

"This game broke my leg. I've been stuck in this corner since I got here."

"How do we get out?"

"I have no idea, but I think it'll stop when someone manages to get the orb. Seems impossible, though."

"How long have you been here?" I ask.

"Not sure. It was noon when I got here."

"You've been here for twenty hours!?"

"Has it been that long?"

"It was eight in the morning when I found the device that brought me here," I say.

"I found one of those too. It was in a coffee shop downtown. My dad was taken by the Thorn, so I set out to find the orb," Brett says.

"I found mine in the clock tower in the downtown park. I think my mom was taken by the Thorn too."

I feel bad for Brett. I know what he's going through when it comes to his dad, and he's been here for nearly a day. On top of that, he's been stuck in this corner the whole time. I can't imagine how helpless he must be feeling.

"Alright, explain how this thing works," I say.

"Well, the tornado acts nothing like a real tornado. It doesn't suck anything into it, just forces things away. Even though it moves around the orb, the wind is strongest on this side. Make it to the left or right wall, and you have a chance. The far wall is the least windy. If you jump from there, you should be able to grab the orb. None of these three have tried it, though. Those two have been fighting for a while now, and one of them is bound to give up at any moment. That other guy with the tattoos has been here the longest, jumping from wall to wall. Stay away from him because he'll fight you if you get in his way."

"Thanks for the advice."

"No problem… Lylon, I'm out of this, but you've got a chance. I know you can do this."

"Hey, I'm sorry for what's happened to you," I say, nodding my head. Sadly, I know exactly what he must be feeling.

"Don't be. Just grab the orb, and this nightmare will end. Good luck."

As soon as the twister moves to the other side of the room, I force my way up. The wind is still very strong, making me slip. Taking a deep breath, I throw myself forward, trying to get far, but I land on my face and get forced back. The tornado rounds the corner again, so I have to wait.

I watch the man with the tattoos jump and miss the orb, only to be thrown against the other wall. The left wall is now clear, so I make my move. I crawl my way toward it, keeping low to avoid the wind as much as possible. It works for the most part, but the wind is still very strong. I manage to force my way to the next wall and crawl towards the center. When I move to stand, I notice that the tornado is about to head my way. I wait for it to pass, but I see the exact moment when one of the guys fighting goes limp and gets thrown against the far wall. Now the man with the tattoos and the other guy are the two fighting.

The tornado passes around onto their side, so I crawl to the center. When I'm close, I throw my whole body forward and reach for the orb. But I'm not even close to grabbing it, and I'm thrust to the other wall right in the middle of the brawl. I hit my head but manage to duck down and crawl between the legs of one of them. I now have an idea.

Glancing at Brett, I try to bring his words into my mind. He told me the wind is not very strong on the wall with the door, so I head for that side. When I get about four feet close, something grabs my foot, and I start to slip backward. I look behind me to find the man with the tattoos grasping my ankle. I struggle against his hold, trying to break free, but he doesn't budge.

"Get off of me!" I scream.

I kick as hard as I can, and I manage to land a blow on his nose. With a grunt, he releases my foot and slides backward out of reach. I turn back and crawl a little more but feel the wind beat against my chest and skin. It burns to breathe it in because of how hard it's blowing. I force myself forward some more, and I'm a few feet away before I slip again. With all my might, I lunge forward and crash to the far wall.

I made it.

Brett was right. Now that I'm on the far wall, crawling to the center is easier. On this side, the wind isn't nearly as strong. More like a nice breeze than the monsoon on the other walls.

I let the tornado pass by my side of the room. Time for my idea. I start to army crawl towards the orb, and once I'm only a few feet away, I stop. The tornado is heading my way again, and when it swirls on this side, I lunge forward, using its force to take me to the orb. Reaching out, I snatch the orb out of the air and land on my side as I skid to a stop.

I look up at my extended arms and open my hands to find the glowing ball of energy. The orb sends jolts of electricity through my veins as a low, peaceful hum fills my ears. I let out a sigh of relief. The wind and tornado stop, and an eerie silence settles.

I got it! I actually got it!

Smiling, I turn around to find a fist connect with my jaw. My head jolts backward and I double over in pain as the tangy taste of blood floods my mouth. I spit, and a tooth falls to the ground. Dazed, I look up to find the bald man with the tattoo sleeve towering over me.

"Thanks for stopping the wind for me. Made it much easier to get the orb," he says.

I look around the room, but there's no one else here. Were they teleported back? If that's the case, why was this man left here with me? He should've been teleported too. The orb is on the ground in front of me, out of reach. I must've dropped it when he punched me. The man bends down and grabs it.

"Pl—Please! M—My mom was taken," I manage to say between sobs.

"You think what happened to your mother is my problem? My wife was killed. I need this orb, and I'm going to use it." The man brings the orb to his mouth and whispers, "I wish my wife would be brought back."

The moment he finishes his wish, the orb stops glowing, looking like a normal marble, but in the blink of an eye, it bursts, falling apart into millions of pieces of dust. The dust twists in a circle and flies up until there's nothing left. It worked, but I didn't use it.

"No, no, no!" I cry.

"That was pretty cool, wasn't it, kid? Thanks again for making it easy for me. Now I need to get home to my wife. Good luck, kid," he says with a maniacal laugh and disappears.

I had it. It was in my hands, but I let it get away. I found it, but someone took it. It's like I've lost Mom all over again, but there's no way to bring her back this time. I've lost my chance to tell her how much I love her and how much she means to me. I won't get to give her a hug or spend any more time with her.

This time she's gone for good.

My head is spinning, and I feel nauseous as I sob on the metal floor. I feel defeated, with blood pouring out of my mouth and my knee swelling with pain from when I hit it entering the room.

Little by little, the world drifts away until I'm surrounded by utter darkness.

Chapter Thirteen

6:40 PM

At some point, I teleported back to the clock tower. I don't know how long I've been lying on the ground. Pain radiates from every pore of my being as I drift in and out of consciousness. A voice reaches my ears, and I hope it's an angel telling me I'm dead. I feel dead. I feel like a failure. I've failed Dad, failed myself, and Mom. All I had to do was wish for her return, and she would be here right now.

"Lylon!" someone calls from outside.

I'm too tired and in too much pain to respond or even move. I decide to just lie here, but the voice doesn't let me.

"Lylon, get up!"

"Maybe he's dead," a second voice says.

"He's not dead. I can see him breathing, but he's badly hurt." Both voices sound familiar.

"Dave, help me sit him up," says the first voice.

Dave? The football jock from school? The one that bullies all the nerds and picks on me for not doing his homework? Why is he here? I guess the better question is, who is he with?

I open my eyes and am blinded by the sun. But if the sun is shining through the door, it means it's setting. Could I have been unconscious the whole day? I force my eyes open and find Charlie staring down at me.

"Lylon! Are you okay?" he asks.

"Dude, you look like you've been hit by a bus," Dave says from behind Charlie.

"It's because I have," I mumble.

My jaw hurts, and I can still taste blood, but my knee is somewhat better. My back is on the ladder. Reaching down, I pull up my left pant leg and find my entire kneecap purple. I don't think it's broken, but I won't know for sure until I try to walk on it. Charlie crouches down beside me and hands me a water bottle from my backpack. I gulp down the entire thing and put my head back against the ladder. Dave and Charlie are staring at me, both wearing the same clothes from yesterday.

"Never thought I would see you two hanging out together," I croak. My voice is weak, and when I cough into my elbow, a little blood comes out.

"Yeah, well, our parents are dead, so I guess we gotta stick together," replies Dave.

"Our?" I ask as I glance at Charlie.

"Dave is my stepbrother," he replies.

"Neither one of us wanted it to happen, but it did. My dad and his mom just had to get married. Pathetic. They should've stayed single," Dave says.

It makes sense. The reason Charlie gets it the worst from Dave. I only wonder why they kept it a secret.

"Why didn't you tell me?" I ask.

"We didn't tell anyone. We hated each other so much we wanted nothing to do with each other. A few months after I was born, my dad passed from cancer, and his mom left when he was a baby. Then my mom met his dad a couple years ago, and the rest is history," Charlie says.

"How'd you two find me anyway?" I ask.

"Some bad stuff went down, man. We were at home about an hour ago when a Thorn soldier burst down our front door. My dad and his mom blocked them from getting to us and told us to run. We ran out the back door. Our house is in the neighborhood on the other side of this park, so we came here. When we saw the door open, we decided to explore, and here we are," Dave says.

"Your parents might not be dead. Maybe they were spared."

"They're dead. We… we heard the cannons and their screams… they're gone," Charlie says.

We sit here in silence, deep in thought. There's been too much killing and loss. Will it ever end? I realize I don't have it as bad as others. Charlie and Dave have lost both of their parents. I've only lost one. At least, as far as I know at the moment.

"So, what happened to you?" Dave asks.

I tell them everything. When I finish, I'm out of breath, and Charlie gives me another bottle of water from my backpack. This time I drink it more slowly.

"What a jerk. I mean, I can be a jerk, but that guy takes the cake," Dave says.

"So, this is the device that teleported you to the orb?" Charlie asks, picking up the object.

"Yeah, this is it."

Charlie fiddles around with it and even presses the button, but nothing happens. Concluding it's now worthless, he tosses it back to the ground.

Dave moves away from the doorway, and I catch another glimpse of the sun.

"What time is it?" I ask as I struggle to get up.

Charlie looks at his watch. "Six fifty. Why?"

Shoot! Dad will be beside himself with worry, and I have no idea what has happened to Valerie. I need to get moving, but everything hurts. Putting my hands on the ground, I try to force myself up but fail. Charlie and Dave grab my arms and help me up, and I try to put weight on my left leg, but it shoots up in pain. My head starts spinning, and I feel like I'm going to pass out again, but I take deep breaths in an effort to keep my senses. I need to stay off my left leg as much as possible, but that will be a challenge.

"Your knee good?" Dave asks.

"It hurts, but it's manageable," I say.

It's not the complete truth, but we need to get going. Despite my mom being a nurse and teaching me some stuff, it doesn't take much to figure out if something is broken, which my knee is not. I can walk if I need to, but it'll take longer to heal. If I can get a brace, I should be fine as long as I don't try to carry anything.

"We need to get to my house. My dad should be back, and he'll know what to do."

"Are you sure he'll be there?" Charlie asks.

"He'll be there," I say.

He has to be. I bet Valerie is back already, but whether or not my dad came to look for us is a different story. He might not be there, but I'm still going to believe he is.

I put my left arm around Dave's neck, and he puts his right arm around my back to help me walk. We stumble the first couple of steps, but once outside, we find our rhythm. Basically, I'm hopping on my right foot with my left leg bent back off the ground. It honestly isn't that hard. I remember doing one-legged hops in physical education class when I was in kindergarten. It feels just like yesterday when I left elementary school for middle school. I remember vividly walking through the halls on the last day of fifth grade, saying goodbye to all my teachers. I miss how easy life was then.

We continue down the concrete pathway that leads out of the park, past the changing trees and the leaves all over the ground. It'll be a while until I return. If I return. The thought makes me a little sad. This is mine and Valerie's favorite place, but we won't come back for a while. Not until the Thorn leave. If they leave.

We make it to the park exit, and Charlie stops and looks at me.

"You're gonna have to direct us because I have no idea where you live."

"We need to go into that neighborhood," I say, pointing in front of me. "I'll show you from there."

"Never thought I'd go to your house," Dave says.

"And I never thought you'd help anyone other than yourself, so we both thought wrong."

"Oh, how the turns have tabled," Dave says.

"You mean how the tables have turned," Charlie corrects him.

"Yeah, whatever."

We cross the street but stay on the sidewalk. I would like to weave between houses, but it'll be difficult with my leg. With our newfound knowledge of the Thorn being able to cloak themselves, I doubt it would make any difference anyway.

We continue on the sidewalk with Dave helping me walk. His neck is sweaty, and my arm slips out, causing me to stumble. Dave reaches out and catches me before I fall face-first onto the concrete. We stop for a moment, and I wipe my arm off while Dave wipes off his neck before walking again.

"Thanks," I say.

"Don't mention it," he says.

"I'm sorry, by the way," I tell him.

"For what?"

"For your parents. I didn't tell you back there, but I am."

"Don't be. I mean, yeah, it sucks, and I will miss them. I will even miss his mom," he says, nodding at Charlie walking ahead of us. "I don't know, I guess we all have parent issues right now, huh?"

"Yeah… I guess so." I stay silent for a moment. "You know… I don't think you're an idiot. Just lazy."

He cracks a small smile, then wipes it away. We walk for a little longer before he breaks the silence once more.

"I don't think you'd be a horrible athlete. I think you'd be an unreal running back."

"Ha! Too bad I've always wanted to try tennis."

He snorts. "Tennis!?"

"Yeah! It looks interesting."

"Well, at least it's not golf."

"You're not so bad," I say.

"Neither are you," he says.

If someone had told me a week ago that I'd be having this conversation with Dave, I would have laughed. Until yesterday, I hated the guy, and now we're having normal conversations like normal people. I didn't think in a million years that would happen, but I'm honestly glad it did. All it took was an alien invasion to get us on the same page. Up ahead, Charlie stops at an intersection.

"Continue straight one mo—"

"Shh," he stops me.

Dave and I pause behind him. At first, I don't hear anything, but then metal clanking reaches my ears, coming from down the street. It's very quiet and distant, but it's getting closer. I grab ahold of Charlie and pull him backward, and we all turn around and hurry to the house we just passed.

Out of breath, we crouch behind the bushes and try to listen, keeping our eyes on the road. The clanking stops only to be replaced by a shrilling noise, like fingernails on a chalkboard. We all wince at the sound, which continues to grow louder until the source rounds the corner.

A lone Thorn soldier, dragging his six-foot cannon behind him, emerges from the street up ahead. He picks up the cannon and starts walking straight to us. There's no way he saw us. How does he know we're here? It doesn't matter. We won't get to find out.

Suddenly a second Thorn soldier appears right in front of the bushes, and we don't have time to react. The Thorn that just appeared grabs Charlie's thin arm with his big meaty hand and yanks him from the bushes so hard his arm rips completely off and starts gushing with blood.

Charlie flies through the air and hits the tree in the yard headfirst with a crack. Charlie's body goes limp, and Dave and I scream in horror. The Thorn soldier is towering over us with arms bigger than my body and eyes that look like an eclipse. He has that same toothy grin as the leader on TV, but his black teeth are stained with blood. Human blood.

The Thorn soldier throws Charlie's arm at Dave, pulls out his cannon, and takes one shot. Dave shrieks as his skin begins to melt. The smell of burning flesh fills the air and flares up my nostrils making me nauseous. Dave screams in agony as his skin bubbles and drips off his body like a melting popsicle. The Thorn soldier bellows out a laugh as Dave slowly dies. All I can do is watch in horror.

This is it. This is where I die.

The Thorn soldier looks at me, but his cannon is lowered. "You weak humans disgust me." His deep, menacing voice rattles my bones. "Now, run."

I don't need to be told twice. Despite pain shooting in my knee, I stumble to my feet and take off as fast as I can. I run back between the houses and straight towards my house, the adrenaline pumping through my body, numbing my pain as I go.

I need to get home.

I need to find my dad.

I need help.

Chapter Fourteen

7:15 PM

Tears stream down my face as I run. I want to break down and cry, but I have to keep moving. Charlie was a good kid, and they tore his arm off and smashed his head into a tree. I finally made things right with Dave, and they burned off all his skin while he was still alive. I can't get their screams out of my head.

The pain in my knee catches up to me, and I stop running. I look down at myself, and my clothes are covered in blood. Blood from my mouth and Charlie's arm getting ripped off. My eyes burn. Why did they spare me? What did Charlie or Dave do to deserve such a horrible fate? I can't take this anymore. Everyone I'm encountering is dying. If Charlie and Dave hadn't found me, they might have lived.

Could this all be my fault? My mom, Charlie, and Dave? I feel horrible. Two days ago, I wished Dave would drop dead, and he just did. I just got onto Dave's good side and felt like he could be a friend. Then, five minutes later, he gets brutally murdered. Am I next? When will all these killings stop?

Emerging from between two houses, I round the corner. My house is right down the street. The sun has set now, and it's starting to get a little chilly.

Soon, I'll be home, I think, and this is what gets me going.

I hope Valerie and Dad are there. I don't know what I'm more afraid of, them not being there or finding out something happened to them while I was gone. I just need my dad. And Valerie.

I continue to limp down the street. My mouth is still very sore, but for the most part, the pain has gone down. My gums have finally stopped bleeding from where the tooth is missing, and the hole feels like shredded meat against my tongue. I keep trying not to touch it, but my tongue keeps poking it. I'm never going to get a fake tooth. The gap will serve as a reminder. A reminder of how I failed to save my mom when she was in my grasp. I'll never forgive myself for that.

As soon as I make it to my house and limp up the driveway, the front door swings open. I get to the porch, and Dad rushes out and yanks me inside, unaware of my knee injury. I yelp in pain as he closes and locks the door behind us. I expect him to be furious with me, but instead, he pulls me into a tight hug.

"Shh. It's okay, Lylon. You're okay, son."

"N—No! I failed!" I cry.

"No, you didn't. You have nothing to be ashamed of."

"No, Dad, you don't understand! I had it! The orb. It was in my hands!" He pulls away from me for a second and looks down at me. "All I had to do was wish and Mom would be here. But this man beat me and used it! Mom's never coming back!"

My legs give out and I collapse to the floor. Dad immediately kneels by my side and hugs me tightly, making me cry even harder.

I don't know how long we sit on the floor before my crying subsides. I wipe the tears off my cheeks, but more stream down my face, so I just leave them. Dad is rubbing my back and that somewhat calms me, but I can't shake off the feeling that I've just gone through a blender. My leg is extended, and I'm afraid to move it.

Finally, Dad looks at me with teary eyes. "When I got to the hospital, it was empty. There was one nurse left, her name was Janice. Your mom wasn't killed… she was taken… Regardless, it's not your fault. You can't blame yourself for anything."

"But I could've brought her back. I had the orb… it was in my hand," I say with a sniffle.

"Where's Valerie?" he asks.

"She's not here!?" I'm immediately worried. If she isn't here, then that means she ran into trouble of her own. We never should've split up.

"No. The note you left said she went with you… Did she not?"

"She did, but we split up. If she's not here th—then she's still out there! We have to go look for her." I try to stand, but my limbs refuse to obey me.

"Hold on a second, Lylon. What happened to you?" Dad asks, taking stock of my injuries for the first time.

"Before we lost the broadcast on the TV, it showed the clock tower in the downtown park. At the top of the tower was a glow, and I thought it was the orb. Valerie and I left this morning, but she wanted to go to her house to see if her parents had returned, so I went to the park by myself. When I got inside the clock tower, the orb wasn't there, but I found a device that transported me to a room. It had its own weather system, and a mini tornado was twirling around the room while a few people were fighting for the orb. I bruised my knee on the way in, but managed to get the orb, but then a big man… this man beat me and took the orb." I stop as a shudder overtakes my body at the memory of that brute beating me. "He knocked a tooth out when he punched my jaw. I lost consciousness for several hours, and when I woke up, I was back in the clock tower and Charlie and Dave found me. They helped me up, and we were on our way here, but… we ran into some

Thorn. They can cloak themselves, so we didn't see them. They… they killed them both."

I can't take this anymore. All the death and destruction are too much to handle.

As I calm down from narrating the day's events, I notice *it* for the first time. I've been too busy crying and thinking about how bad I failed everyone to notice the German Shepherd lying on the floor a few feet away.

"Whose dog is that?"

"Don't know. I found him when I was out, and he followed me. I thought it might be good to have an extra set of eyes and ears to protect the house. He's very well trained. His name is Rudy… I wanted to look for you, but I thought you might return. I decided to wait, and if you didn't show up when it got dark, I would set out to look."

"I guess I came back just in time."

"Yeah."

We sit in silence for a little while. Rudy gets up and comes over to sniff me and begins licking my face. He sits down next to me, and I scratch behind his ears. I've always wanted a dog. I wonder what my dad went through out there, but I don't want to ask.

"Why did they spare me?" I finally ask.

"What do you mean?"

"The Thorn. They… they killed Dave and Charlie but let me go. The Thorn soldier told me to run. Why? Who decides who lives and dies? Nothing is making any load of sense!" I say, and my eyes well again.

"I wish I knew Lylon! Nothing of what's happening is fair, but you can't blame yourself. I don't care if you lost a wishing orb and you're not responsible for what happened to your mom, Charlie, or Dave. And I'm proud of you for trying. I love you no matter what. Okay?"

I nod. "Okay."

Dad really believes it isn't my fault, otherwise he would tell me. I know I failed, but I don't want to argue. He gets up and walks out of the room, but I remain on the floor, deflated. I'll never forget this day.

A couple of minutes later, Dad comes back with a bag of ice, painkillers, and a knee brace. I dry-swallow two pills and put the ice on my knee. I'll put the brace on after I finish icing.

"Valerie is still out there. We need to find her," I say.

"Yeah. We'll find her."

"I'm not letting you go without me. We go together. I don't care how bad my knee hurts; you're not leaving me here."

"I never said you were staying here. From now on, we stick together. You are not leaving my side. We need to find Valerie and Anesh. We haven't talked to him since yesterday, and we need to make sure that both he and his mother are all right."

I nod. "When are we leaving?"

"When you finish icing, take Rudy outside, and I'll get some stuff together to leave."

"Okay."

I ice for a little longer and then put the brace on. Standing up is more difficult than I thought, but dad helps me. When I finally get up, I walk around, and it feels better. I still feel soreness, but for the most part, the pain is gone. I'll have to keep icing it if possible, but I might not always have a supply of ice.

"How's your knee?" Dad asks.

"Way better. I probably shouldn't run, but walking shouldn't be an issue."

I call Rudy and he follows me to the back door.

The cool night air feels good, and I close my eyes to savor this rare moment of calmness. I try to imagine that it's a few days earlier. Before the world fell. Back when my most serious problem was that I was overloaded with all AP homework, and I wasn't in the mood to tackle it. Back to when I would hang out with Anesh or take Valerie for a walk in the park or movie night. Life will never be the same.

My mind then drifts to Valerie. She's in trouble, and we have no way of finding her. There's no reason for her to not be here unless she's run into trouble. Neither of us should have been out past noon, considering how early we left. I'm troubled at the thought that she might not be all right.

Finally, my thoughts go to Mom. I already feel guilty for telling her I had other plans on the only day she had off. Now I feel guilty for losing the orb when I had it. Just one sentence and she would be here.

Rudy brushes against me, and I'm brought back to the present. He's finished with his business, so I start for the door when I hear talking. Rudy tries to push ahead of me, but I grab his collar and stop him. I tiptoe inside the house. Dad is talking to someone at the front door. Rudy starts to growl and I shush him.

"I'm sure we can work something out," Dad says.

"Nope. We can't. Tell me. Are you home alone?" the man asks. His voice sounds familiar.

Tentatively, I peek around and make out a bald man with a tattoo sleeve on his arm. The man that stole the orb from me.

"Yeah. I'm alone."

This isn't a friendly conversation. Dad never lies.

"Good," the man says.

The gunshot pierces through my eardrums as my heart sinks into my stomach. Bolting around the corner, I see Dad falling to the floor, clutching his chest. The man is gone, the only evidence of him being here is the gun he must have dropped when he took off. I run to Dad, drop down beside him, and immediately apply pressure to the wound.

"No, no, no, no! Dad! Please no!" I say between sobs.

Dad is lying wounded and helpless, and I can't help him. He lifts his bloody hand and caresses my cheek. He's fading away.

"Please don't go! I love you! I need you!"

"Y—you have to be strong. Ly—Lylon… I lo—love you. Don't y—you forget it."

Chapter Fifteen

7:45 PM

I rest my head on Dad's chest, surrendering to the pain that threatens to rip my heart out. Now both of my parents are gone. This monster shattered my life for the second time today.

What should I do now?

Valerie. Only she would know what to say to me. I'll have to go look for her on my own, and I should probably try to find Anesh if he's still out there. And what about Dad? I can't just leave his body lying in the doorway, but I can't take him to a cemetery either. He needs a proper burial, but I can't do that. Perhaps I should bury him in the backyard. It won't be the best place for him, but I need to bury him, and this might be my only chance. After I set out for Valerie, I can't come back. The man who stole the orb somehow found us and shot Dad, which means this place is no longer safe.

I close and bolt the door, wondering why Dad opened it in the first place. Maybe he saw someone coming and thought it was Valerie. But whatever his reason, I'll never get to find out unless I get another orb and bring him back.

I want to know how that man found us. I didn't know who he was before he stole the orb from me, and even then, he still didn't know me. It doesn't make sense that he'd come to kill my dad, especially after taking the orb from me. Why would he even do it?

Picking up the gun the man left behind, I tuck it in the waistband of my jeans. I look down and I'm disgusted at how much blood is on me. My clothes are soaked with blood from three different people, my arms are covered, and I can feel dried blood all over my face. I'll have to clean up later.

Rudy's sitting at my dad's feet, resting his head on them, whining. It's as if he knows my dad is dead and not coming back. His sad eyes are directed at me and I feel tears running down my cheeks. I've never lost a family member before, but now I'm losing everyone.

Rudy follows me as I go to the garage to get a shovel and a tarp. He's no longer wagging his tail and his head is down. He's as sad as I am. I cover Dad with the tarp, unable to look at his dead body. I can't face reality and see another person who means so much to me dead.

I go to the backyard with Rudy in tow. It's a full moon, and clouds start to move in. I really hope it doesn't rain. I start to dig the perfectly cut grass and toss the dirt into a pile next to me. It might take me a while to dig a hole big enough, but I'm in no rush. I need to find Valerie, but this is my only chance to say goodbye to my dad. I didn't get the chance with my mom.

At first, Rudy just watches me, but then he comes over and starts digging with me. He probably has no idea why I'm digging, but I'll take the extra help. Every few minutes I take a second to catch my breath and rest my knee. It burns from the movement, but I put it to the back of my mind and focus on the task at hand. My shovel hits a big rock with a clank, and I have to crouch down to dig it out.

The rock is about the size of my head and so heavy I struggle to pick it up. Once it's out of the way, I resume digging. At this point, the hole is only big enough for Rudy to fit into. I never thought I'd ever dig a hole to bury a human body, but I didn't think a lot of things would happen.

Almost two hours later, the hole is almost finished, and Rudy stops digging and lies down, panting. I don't blame him. My arms burn, my knee aches, and I'm tired and sweating. The light is not enough, so I walk back to the house to retrieve a headlamp. When I get inside, I notice that the blood all over me makes my sweat turn a tint of red. I really want to clean up, but I have more important matters to deal with.

I stop and look at the tarp over my dad's body. It'd be easier if I just went ahead and took him outside, so I walk over to him and take the tarp off. I grab his hands and I shiver at the thought of touching a dead person. It's a weird feeling, so I quickly drag his body through the house, leaving behind a trail of blood.

I try to look away, the evidence of my father's death making my stomach churn. I shouldn't have to do this right now. What would have happened if Dad hadn't lied? Would the man have spared him, or would he still have killed Dad? Did the man even know he was killing my dad?

When I get to the backyard, Rudy is next to the mound of dirt we created, and the moment he sees Dad's body, he whimpers. Shaking my own tears away, I set his body down next to the hole and pick up the shovel. The hole is long enough, but it needs to be a little deeper, so I resume digging, and once it's about three feet deep, I climb up and rest with my legs dangling over the edge.

Under normal circumstances, this would be a nice night. It's the perfect temperature, and the stars are everywhere. You usually don't see too many stars in the big city, but with most of the lights out downtown, there are so many. I wish I could just lie under them with Valerie by my side, but I can't.

I get up and walk over to my dad's body. This time I grab him by his shirt so I don't touch his lifeless skin, and I drag him until he falls into the hole. His body hits the ground with a thud, making me wince. I might be physically hurt, but no pain compares to what I feel inside. I'm glad for Rudy's presence keeping an eye out for me, but it's not the same as having another person.

I pick up the shovel and start to push all the dirt from the mound back into the hole. Once it's filled, I toss the shovel and my headlamp and plop onto the ground. I might not have anyone to talk to, but I start talking anyway.

"Why did you open the door? You had to have seen who it was, right? So why would you open it?" I stay silent for a moment, but I have more to say. "Dad, I don't know what to do! How do I go on? I'm losing everyone!"

Sobs rack my entire body as the realization of what has happened sinks in. When I finally calm down, tears are still in my eyes, and I don't know if they'll ever go away.

"I want to be strong like you said, but how can I? How am I supposed to survive a game of chance?"

What did I just say? A game of chance. What if the Thorn aren't just here for resources? Maybe they're here for something else. The orbs, them walking among us cloaked, the randomness of deaths. Something doesn't seem right, but just like everything else, I doubt I'll get the answer.

I sit in silence and think about all the memories I have with Mom and Dad. We were a team, us three. I remember when my dad taught me how to ride a bike and how he used to help me with my math homework until I got way better at math than him in the fifth grade. I remember when my mom worked less and would go on school trips with me in elementary school and how she taught me how to drive. Family vacations and celebrations come to mind, and I smile sadly. I'll never get them back.

I look at my dad's pathetic grave and frown. I might not be able to buy him a gravestone, but there's something else I can do. On the wall in our kitchen, there's a bunch of crosses Mom has collected. Her favorite is the one Dad had made for her out of sticks and twine, then painted a dark brown color. It's my favorite too, and it's perfect for what I need.

I plant the cross right at the head of Dad's grave, and it might not be proper, but it's the best I can do. I pull the gun out of my waistband and plop back down next to the grave.

"Thank you for everything. I hope I'll make you proud," I sniffle.

At this point, the only thing I can do is try to make both my parents proud. I'm sitting with the gun in my hand and my arms resting on my knees when something creaks to my left. I look up and see a shadow at the wooden side gate of the backyard. My heart beats loudly as I raise the gun, ready to protect myself and my home.

"Lylon? Put the gun down. It's me."

Chapter Sixteen

Valerie

My parents are gone. I wasn't expecting to find that out, but here I am, lying on the floor with my back against the kitchen island sobbing. Now I understand how Lylon feels about his mom and why it's important to find the orb. I only wish there was one for me to find. But there's not, and I didn't even get to say goodbye to Mom and Dad. They didn't even die to the Thorn, they died in a car wreck. To be honest, though, if they were to die, I would rather it be that than suffer at the hands of the Thorn.

I need to go to Lylon. I'm grateful I still have him and his father to look after me. They're good people, and I'm sure we'll get through this together. Will Lylon be back from the clock tower? There's no doubt in my mind he'll find the orb. He's strong, smart, and resourceful. I still wish there were a second one, but at the same time, I don't. Who would I use it for? Mom or Dad? How am I supposed to choose between my parents? I love them both equally.

"Valerie? Are you here?" a voice calls out from the front door.

I didn't hear anyone enter, but I was too busy thinking about my parents. More like crying that they are gone. The voice is familiar, and I realize it is Carly's, a friend of mine from school. I realize I'm not in any danger, so I stand up, looking around. The front door is wide open, but there's no one in sight.

Slowly, I creep toward the door when Carly appears right in front of me. My heart skips a beat and I jump backward screaming.

"Shh. Don't want to alert any Thorn in the area," she says, straightening her glasses.

"H—how did… what?!"

"I'm using one of their cloaking devices," Carly says.

"What are you talking about?" I ask.

"You don't know?"

"Know what? Just tell me!" I respond.

"Okay, okay. The Thorn can turn invisible. Well, I've got one of their cloaking devices."

Under normal circumstances, I wouldn't believe that anyone can turn invisible. But these aren't normal circumstances. Now I get why we haven't seen too many Thorn soldiers around.

"It makes sense, but how did you get one?" I ask.

"I'm not telling you. It's a secret," Carly says.

"Seriously? Carly, I am not in the mood! I just found out my parents are dead."

"Oh my God! I'm so sorry. I had no idea. Was… it the Thorn?"

"No. It was a car crash on their way back from their vacation. The sheriff of some town in Colorado left me a voice message," I say, and my eyes start to water again.

"I'm so sorry, Valerie. Really, I am… You need to come with me."

"Go with you where?"

"Grab my hand, and I'll explain. We aren't safe here."

Taking her hand, we move to the closet door, and I frown. We stand in front of the mirror, but we're not reflected in the glass. Except I can see her and the energy field around us. It's a transparent barrier that reminds me of a bubble, but nobody on the outside can see in. Only now do I note that Carly holds a metal box containing a switch with strange symbols engraved on it.

"Flipping this switch turns anything touching it that's animate invisible. It also creates a sound barrier, so whatever we say here isn't heard out there. It's very cool technology, but we have no idea how it works," Carly says.

"We?"

Carly starts walking toward the front door and I follow. Once we're outside and walking down the street, she answers my question.

"We as in around thirty people. We have a community of survivors just on the outskirts of Dallas. We're currently housed in a hotel that has plenty of food and water. We plan to stay there until these awful Thorn leave our planet. That's where we're headed."

"If we're headed there right now, we need to get Lylon and his dad."

"They're alive?" she asks, surprised.

"Yeah. I've been at their house this whole time. I was going to meet Lylon back there later."

"It's strange your boyfriend let you come here on your own."

I shake my head. "It was all my idea. Lylon went to find the orb at the clock tower, and I came here to see if there was any news about my parents."

"Lylon went to look for an orb? Why?"

"Because we saw the hospital get raided on TV. His mom was either taken or killed and he wants her back."

"His mom is gone? That's horrible. She's a very sweet person. If she was taken, I can't imagine what they put her through."

"Yeah, me neither," I mumble.

"Look… I don't want to sound rude, but we need to get to the community. I know Lylon means a lot to you, but you have to trust me."

"I can't just leave him."

"I'm not asking you to leave him, but for now, you should really come with me."

"Fine. But this better be good."

We leave my house and walk for thirty minutes out of my neighborhood and down the highway near my house. I've never seen all six lanes of the highway piled up with cars. I can't believe the mess we are in. I look up and still see the massive alien warship overhead, casting a shadow over ninety percent of the city. How did they make a ship that big that can fly? I look at Carly next to me, still holding my hand to make sure we stay cloaked.

"So, how did you manage to get your hands on one of these?"

"We took down a Thorn soldier," she answers.

"Really? How did you manage that?"

"I'm kidding. Actually, we just found it. Well, actually, this guy in our group, Ryan, found it."

"How'd you learn how to use it, though?"

"Ryan told us about it. He said he saw a group of Thorn pull them out and use them. Then he found one in a twenty-car pileup downtown. He thinks a Thorn might've dropped it or something. Oh, another thing you should know about these is that we can still see other Thorn cloaked, and they can see us. So, if one comes around the corner, we'll be able to see them."

"Well, it might not be complete invisibility, but at least we'll see them," I say positively.

We walk for another hour before we exit the highway and turn onto an empty street. The image of desolation is heart-wrenching. Destroyed cars, stores missing windows, and even a collapsed building. Newspapers are floating in the wind, and the sight really reminds me of the stereotypical apocalypse. We take another right turn and end up on a street that looks a little nicer than the last. At the end of the street, I see a four-story hotel that looks unscathed.

"Is that it?" I ask Carly.

"Yes," she replies.

Once outside the door, Carly turns off the cloaking device, and I let go of her hand. She knocks once and then twice in succession. We wait a moment before the door slides open. The inside is very damp and dimly lit. The windows have black paper taped over them or black curtains to block any light from escaping. Carly and I walk toward a group of people playing cards in the lobby. The woman behind the front desk smiles at us as we walk by.

"She watches over the place and lets people in after they go on runs. We've been here since day one. Come on, my mom wants to see you," Carly says.

We enter a large conference room in the middle of which there's a large table with twenty chairs or so. At the head of the table, Carly's mom, Tris, is talking to a boy of about eighteen. They're looking at a map, so I assume they're planning on looking for more supplies.

Tris sees us and smiles. "Valerie! It's so good to see you're okay."

"Oh, Tris! It's good to see you too."

"Carly, can you give the cloaking device to Devon so he can go on his run?" Tris asks her daughter.

The boy, Devon, nods at us after Carly gives him the device and leaves the room. Carly and I approach Tris, and she hugs us.

"I'm glad you made it back in one piece," Tris tells Carly. "Are you hungry, Valerie?"

"Actually, yeah. Last time I ate was dinner last night."

"I'll go get you something," Carly says and leaves the room.

"She's a good friend," I say, and Tris smiles.

A crackling sound comes from behind Tris, and she pulls a walkie-talkie off her waistband and adjusts a nob before setting it on the table.

"Who are you talking to?" I ask.

"There's another community in the center of Dallas somewhere. We don't know each other's exact location, but we're keeping each other in the loop. From what we know, they have more people than us, about fifty."

"So, there are more people out there?"

"Yes, but not many."

Carly returns with a plate of fried chicken and baked beans. As soon as she gives it to me, I sit down and devour the whole thing. The meal isn't one of my favorites, but I'm so hungry it tastes like a fancy dish at a gourmet restaurant. It takes me no time to finish it, and when I look up, they're both staring.

"Sorry. I was hungry."

"I can tell," Tris says. "You run out of food or something?"

"Actually, yes. I've been at Lylon's with him and his dad, and they ran out of food. Travis went on a run to get more."

"I'm sorry he didn't come back," she says.

"No, that's not what happened. At least I hope not. Lylon and I left so I could go to my house and Lylon could go to look for the orb. But all I found was a message saying my parents died in a car wreck…"

"Oh, Valerie, I'm so sorry," Tris says with a sad look.

"Thank you. I was home when Carly found me and said I needed to come here. So, I did."

"Well, you should've gotten Lylon and Travis to come with you."

Carly's looking at me with wide eyes. She told me I needed to come with her. The cloaking device would have allowed more people to use it, so why did she want to leave Lylon and Travis behind?

"Carly… why did you tell me I needed to come with you?" I ask her with a look of confusion.

"Because… I wanted you off the street, okay? I know it was selfish, but I didn't want to see my best friend die, and the longer we're outside, the bigger chance of that happening."

Frantically, I turn to Tris. "I need to go to Lylon."

"I understand, but I just gave the cloaking device to Devon."

"It's fine. I'll go without it," I say.

"Wait! Valerie, please don't go out there without a cloaking device," Carly pleads.

"Carly, I have to. Look, I shouldn't have come. Thanks for looking out for me, but we should've either gone to look for Lylon and his father, or you should've left me. I have to get back to him," I tell her. I turn and look at Tris, "Thank you for your hospitality and for the food."

"No problem. When you find them come back here, okay?"

"I will. Thank you," I say and walk out of the room.

I need to get moving because it'll be dark before I get back. Maybe everyone is okay, but maybe not. When I get to the front door, a hand grabs my shoulder. I spin around and see Carly.

"Don't try to talk me out of this," I say.

"I'm not going to. Look… I'm sorry, but I just couldn't stand to see someone else I care about die. My dad… he uh… he didn't make it, and I didn't want to lose you too."

"It's okay. It's my fault too. I should've stayed. I was just happy to see you. And I get it. I lost both my parents and didn't even get to say goodbye. I know what it feels like." I say and give her a hug. When we separate, she sighs.

"Please at least wait until Devon returns. We will give you the cloaking device so you can get Lylon and come back. Please wait."

I think for a moment. I know it's not safe outside and that I could run into Thorn. As much as I hate to admit it, Carly is right.

"Fine. I will wait. But, if he isn't back, I'm leaving at sundown," I say sternly.

***

I walk back the way I came, past a collapsed building and back up the highway. Devon still hadn't returned with the cloaking device when it started to get dark, so I decided to go ahead and leave. I decided the dark would be good enough for cover if I stay in the shadows. So far, so good.

I can't believe my closest friend would make me leave Lylon out there. If our roles were reversed, I have no doubt in my mind that I would have helped her find her boyfriend. I guess we just have different viewpoints on that.

The moon shines above me when I finally make it to Lylon's neighborhood. I'm really glad I didn't run into any trouble on the way back. I reach Lylon's house and walk around the side to the gate because it's always unlocked.

The door creaks, and in the blink of an eye, Lylon raises a gun, pointing it straight to my head. Fear consumes me.

The Lylon I know would never act in violence first. No. Something has happened tonight. Something bad.

I take a deep breath. "Lylon?" I say in a gentle voice. "Put the gun down. It's me."

Chapter Seventeen

Lylon

"Valerie!" I cry and throw the gun down.

I bolt over to Valerie and throw my arms around her tightly. I thought I'd have to look for her and didn't think she would come back. She wraps her legs around my hips, and we kiss for what feels like forever. Rudy trots over and starts sniffing Valerie to make sure she's not a threat. Valerie stops kissing me for a moment.

"What happened here?" she asks.

"So, so much," I say and kiss her again.

When we stop for air, we both sit down next to my dad's grave and talk about what happened today.

"My dad… he got shot on the porch," I begin as tears stream down my face. "This man shot him for no reason!"

"Oh my God!" Valerie cries, pulling me into another hug.

I take a moment so I can talk without sobbing.

"The orb wasn't in the clock tower, but I found a Thorn device instead. I was in the clock tower one moment, and the next, I was in some room with four others and the orb, trying to get it. There was a tornado in the room, protecting the orb. I managed to grab it, but… this man that was in there took it from me! I then woke up in the clock tower to Charlie and Dave, and as we were heading back here, the Thorn killed them, and I ran. When I finally got back here, the guy that took the orb killed my dad on the porch! I don't know why, though! How did he even get to us? He took the orb and then my dad! I feel like I'm losing my mind!"

"Oh, Lylon! I'm so sorry! That must have been awful. I'm sorry I wasn't here."

Valerie gives me a moment to calm down, and I try to get my erratic breathing under control. I wipe my eyes on my shirt.

"What happened with you?" I ask.

"My house was looted. There were two messages on the answering machine. The first one was from my… parents telling me they were on their way." She stops with a sad smile, shaking her head as tears well into her eyes. "The second message was from the police station in Pueblo… they got in a car wreck and didn't make it."

My heart aches. I pull Valerie into a hug.

"Val, I—I'm so sorry."

She buries her face into my chest as she begins to sob. I can't help but cry too. I let her let it all out, and I hold her through everything.

"Carly showed up at my house," she eventually says, sniffling. "You know the Thorn can cloak themselves?"

"Yeah, I saw them do it."

"Well, Carly had one of their devices and used it to bring me to her camp. I wanted to come back for you, but she said it was urgent. I let her take me. Her mom was there along with thirty others, from what she told me. They're at a hotel north of here. Carly wanted me off the streets, but I couldn't stand the thought of leaving you out here alone. I waited until it was dark, then came back here. If I hadn't gone with Carly, I would've been back sooner."

"Valerie… if I'm being honest, I think I would've done the same thing. If I found you and you told me your best friend was out there, I would want you to come back with me. I wouldn't want you out there."

She looks away for a moment, but then she looks back and grabs my hand.

"Lylon, I'm never leaving your side again. We leave together, we make decisions together, and we stay together."

"And I'm never leaving your side. I'll stick with you forever," I promise.

We continue to sit in silence for a little while longer and look up at the stars. They've gotten even brighter, and it looks amazing. The last time I saw stars this bright was when my parents and I drove across the country a couple years ago. We had gone on vacation to Tennessee and drove the whole way. One night, while we were driving, the stars lit up the sky. Tonight reminds me of that night. The only difference is that tonight my parents aren't with me.

Valerie lets go of my hand and stands up. She reaches up to the sky to stretch, and the curve of her back is visible in the moonlight. Bending down, she picks up a handful of dirt and stands at the foot of my father's grave.

"Travis… Lylon's dad… thank you for everything. Thank you for looking after us and for taking me with you when the invasion started. And thank you for being a great father. You might not have been my father, but I know you were a great one for Lylon. I love you like family. You didn't deserve this fate, and I pray you will rest in peace." When she finishes, she drops the dirt on top of my dad's grave and wipes her eyes with her sleeve before coming back to me.

"Thank you," I say.

"It was the truth. Just like your father would tell," she says.

"My dad is dead… but my mom might not be. I've been thinking about this, and I don't know if I should."

"Thinking about what?"

"That I'd rather have my mom be dead for sure. She was taken by the Thorn and is possibly their prisoner. At least Dad will rest now, but Mom will suffer, and I can't bear it. Is it wrong to wish she was dead rather than in the Thorn's hands?"

Valerie looks away and seems to think about this for a moment. I don't expect her to respond, but then she looks me in the eye.

"I don't think it's wrong. If I were in your shoes, I'd wish the same thing. If she were dead, you would have closure, but now you don't know anything, and that's far worse. With your mom, she might be dead, but you have no idea."

It makes me feel a little better knowing that Valerie agrees with me. I still feel guilty for thinking it, but Valerie is right. I'm lucky I have closure for Dad. I might not know how that man found us or why he killed him, but I know he's dead, and I buried him. But Mom… she might float around in space, suffering, or they might have killed her for sport, with me being none the wiser. I have no idea what the Thorn will do with her, which scares me. Mom doesn't have a way of coming back to me.

"We can't stay here any longer," I say.

Valerie nods. "I know."

"I don't want to stay past morning, but I'd prefer if we left tonight."

"We can go to the hotel Carly is staying at."

"That's fine with me, but I'd like to stop by Anesh's house. It's on the way, so we won't be wasting much time."

"Sounds good to me."

Valerie helps me up, and we walk into my house with Rudy following us. Once inside, we head into the kitchen. All the food Dad collected is on the counter, and we divide it evenly between our two backpacks, so we both have enough room for a few clothes. Valerie had grabbed a change of clothes when she was at her house, so she's good.

Grabbing my backpack, I walk into my room and straight to the wardrobe. I take out my favorite pair of jeans, a long-sleeved shirt, and a normal t-shirt and throw them in my bag. I also take a pair of underwear and throw that in my bag as well. Maybe I'll be able to shower off and wash my current clothes once we get to the hotel. I'm still covered in blood, and moving around feels sticky, but I don't have time to clean up.

I give my room one last look. I won't be coming back here anytime soon, if at all. This was the room I grew up in, the one I had for basically my whole life. There are both good and bad memories here that I'll always cherish. Maybe when the Thorn leave, I can come back, but I won't count on it.

When I return to the kitchen, Valerie is bent over, petting Rudy.

"Hey, do you have extra space in your backpack?" Valerie asks.

"Yeah, why?"

"I found a bag of treats and a little bag of dog food. I guess your dad got it when he was at the store."

Nodding, I open my backpack to put the bags inside. The food will give Rudy one meal, so we'll have to find something else for him.

"I'll be right back," I tell Valerie and go to the backyard.

I grab the gun I tossed and tuck it into my waistband. Once again, I stop at the foot of Dad's grave and crouch down.

"This is it, Dad... my final goodbye. Help me be strong to keep us safe. I'm sorry this happened to you. I love you, Dad."

Rudy comes trotting up next to me and looks at the grave. He starts to whine a little, so I scratch behind his ears, and that seems to calm him.

"He's gone Rudy... and he's not coming back. I know you don't understand me, but keep Valerie safe. Protect us, but more importantly, protect her."

Rudy licks my face, and I let him. When I finally stand back up and turn around, I find Valerie at the door.

"Ready?" she asks.

"Yeah, let's go find Anesh."

Chapter Eighteen

10:30 PM

We leave my house, but I don't bother to lock the front door. I have nothing to return to here, and I don't plan on returning. Before leaving, I turn and give the house one last look. While it's not the only house I've lived in, it's the only one I remember.

Valerie, Rudy, and I walk down the driveway and turn left. Anesh's house is less than a five-minute drive, but it'll take us a little longer to get there. It's in the direction of the hotel. I really hope Anesh and his mother are still there. I don't think I can handle losing another person close to me.

The massive warship is just a dark object in the night sky. My neighborhood is in the fifty percent of Dallas that isn't covered by it, although its shadow is cast over us during the day. I can't wait to see that thing leave our atmosphere. How much longer are the Thorn going to stay here? How much more do they need? I'm pretty sure they've taken enough already, but who knows.

"Do you think he'll be there?" Valerie asks as we hurry along the sidewalk holding hands.

"I'm not sure. Hopefully, both he and his mom are there," I say.

"What will we do if he's not there?"

"If he's not there, we'll continue on. As much as I want to find him, I want us to be safe."

It pains me to think about Anesh being hurt or dead. He's been my oldest and closest friend ever since first grade. We always hung out on Friday nights, helped each other with our homework, or talked about girls until I started dating Valerie. We always managed to cheer each other up after a bad day. I love him like a brother, and I don't know what I'd do without him. Then again, I never imagined I'd have to live without my parents, but I have to figure that out now too.

"Tell me something," I say to Valerie.

"What?"

"Considering our odds of survival are completely based on chance, and I might never get to ask, but if I proposed to you, would you say yes?" I ask with a small smile.

"Hmm, I'm not sure. I don't know if I can put up with you for life," she says with a playful gleam in her eyes.

"I guess you'll have to say goodbye to Rudy."

"Oh, if I can't see Rudy, then I guess I would have to say yes." Valerie stays silent for a moment and then looks at me with a serious face. "I would. I told you I'm never leaving your side, and I meant every word."

I smile. Valerie is eighteen, and I'm seventeen, but we both know we'll be together forever. People might say we're too young for such major decisions, but I think it's safe to say that going through an alien invasion together has strengthened our bond. I hope we get the chance.

"So, what will we do besides get married after the Thorn leave?" she asks.

"Don't know, but I'm sure we'll find something to do. Right now, we need to focus on staying alive and keeping each other safe."

"Agreed."

We continue down the sidewalk and turn left at the intersection. Rudy is looking all around us, sniffing everything. I wonder if he can smell or sense a Thorn soldier coming. If that's the case, then Rudy will be really useful to have around.

"You said that when you were cloaked by the device, you could see other Thorn soldiers that are cloaked, right?" I ask Valerie.

"That's what Carly told me, but we didn't run into a Thorn soldier. Why?"

"Because I've been thinking."

"Oh no."

"Just hear me out. Regardless of the Thorn being able to cloak themselves, don't you think we should've seen a lot more of them? I mean, you were in a cloaking device, and you didn't see any of them. They say they're here for resources, but what if they've come here for something else?"

"Maybe because we're in a big city and there aren't many natural resources here. But what else would they be here for?" Valerie asks.

"Well, they started taking people and gave us orbs to bring them back. And the leader said that it would be interesting to watch us try to take them. I was thinking that maybe they're here to test us. He called us *selfish humans*. Sure, they could be here for resources, but I don't think that's the only reason."

Valerie frowns. "It's possible. But why would they want to test us, and for what?"

"I don't know."

We walk a while longer and reach Anesh's street. His house comes into view, and I remember dropping him off here yesterday. So much has happened since then it's hard to believe. I want so badly for him to be here so I can catch up with him, but my optimism evaporates when I see his front door wide open. Every house on the street is either missing windows or has its door kicked in.

"I don't think we'll find him here," Valerie says in a small voice as we walk up the pathway.

"We'll search every room, but we need to be quiet."

Rudy walks into the house and sniffs around. My palms start sweating, and my heart thuds fast in my chest as I pull out a flashlight and turn it on. The front room is a disaster, with a bookshelf knocked over and magazines and papers scattered everywhere. The sofa is torn, the coffee table is smashed, and there's a hole in the flatscreen TV.

Valerie gasps. "What happened in here?"

"Nothing good," I say and continue forward.

We walk into the next room, and the kitchen is even worse. Pots and pans are everywhere, and glass is shattered all over the floor. Rudy is sniffing everything and rushes to Anesh's bedroom. I've been in this house so many times it's shocking to see it like this. The place was always immaculate, not even a dirty dish in the sink, but now, it looks like a bomb went off here.

"They're not here," Valerie whispers.

"No, but they went somewhere."

I shine the light into Anesh's room, and it's not as bad as the rest of the house, but there are still clothes everywhere. Rudy is sniffing a brown shoebox that has tape all over it, and I pick it up.

"What do you think is in there?" Valerie asks as I unwrap it.

"I don't know, but Rudy seems interested in it."

"Maybe it's his stash of drugs," Valerie says as she elbows me.

"No, he's never done drugs," I say, shaking my head.

I hand Valerie the flashlight, and she shines it on the box. I get all the tape off and open the lid. Inside is a sheet of paper and a walkie-talkie. I take both items out and drop the box on the floor.

"Had to flee. If you need me, use the walkie. Anesh," I read out loud my friend's note.

"What are you waiting for? Use it," Valerie says.

I flip the switch to turn the walkie-talkie on. At first, there's no sound, so I turn up the volume, but all I hear is static. I finally press the button to talk.

"Anesh? Are you listening?" I ask.

I wait a moment and get no response. I start to think he either doesn't have the other walkie anymore, or he's gone, but then his voice comes through the speaker.

"Lylon? Is that you?" Anesh asks.

"Yeah, it's me! Valerie's here too!"

"Hey, Anesh!" Valerie says.

"Hey, Valerie! It's so good to hear your voices! I had a feeling you might come to me. Where's your dad?"

I don't want to respond, and Valerie can tell, so she takes the walkie-talkie from me.

"He didn't make it," she says in a low voice. "A lot has happened since we dropped you off. Where are you?" she says.

"I can't tell you where I am, but I can try to get you here. Hold on a minute."

"Where do you think he is?" Valerie asks me.

"I have no idea, but probably with other people if he doesn't want to tell us. He trusts us, but he can't know if anyone else is on the line."

We wait a couple of minutes before Anesh finally comes back on.

"Sorry about that. Like I said, I can't tell you where I am, but we'll try to get you here. You know the downtown park?"

"Yeah," Valerie responds.

"Okay. You need to be there at eleven. Don't be late, or they won't wait for you."

"What time is it right now?" Valerie asks.

"Ten fifty-one. You've got nine minutes. I know that's not much time, but if you hurry, you should get there."

"Oh, one more thing. We have a dog with us," Valerie tells him.

"A dog? Hold on." Anesh goes silent again. "Alright, you're good. And I got your time extended to 11:05."

I take the walkie-talkie from Valerie. "Anesh, what do you want me to do with the walkie?"

"Keep it with you and keep it on. There isn't anyone else I need to get here," he says.

"Okay. We'll see you soon."

"Stay safe. Over and out," Anesh finishes, and I clip the walkie-talkie to my waistband and look over at Valerie.

"We better hurry," I say, and she nods.

We call Rudy and leave through the front door. It's close to 10:55, which gives us ten minutes. It shouldn't take us that long to get to the park from Anesh's house, but I don't want to be left behind, so we go as fast as my limp will allow. I didn't think I would be returning to the park anytime soon, and I kind of don't want to. As much as I like the park, I can't forget what happened to me. Every time I return there from now on, I'll think about how I failed my mom.

Rushing along the sidewalk, we take a couple of turns. We're about halfway to the park when I start to wonder where Anesh is hiding. Considering how secretive the location is, I think we'll be safe there. But Anesh told us to go to the park, and anyone tuned in to our frequency could have heard that and could also show up. That is a chilling thought.

We walk a little more, and eventually, the park comes into view. It's an eerie night. The lamps around are dim, and the metal gate surrounding it makes it look like a graveyard. It's very quiet out here, except for the sound of crickets chirping. We cross the street and stand in front of the park.

"I'm not sure if he wanted us to meet in front of the park or inside," I say.

"Let's wait here," Valerie says, and suddenly Rudy starts to growl.

"Shh, easy Rudy," I tell him, but he doesn't listen, and it makes me think back to when he was sniffing everything.

Maybe he *can* smell Thorn, and maybe there are some very close to us. My breathing stops, afraid that even the rise and fall of my chest might alert the enemy.

And that's when I hear it. A gun clicks three times.

"Don't move," a voice commands from behind us.

Chapter Nineteen

11:05 PM

"Show us your hands," a female voice says.

Valerie and I slowly raise our hands. Our backs are still turned. Rudy growls at them, having adopted a defensive stance. I hope these are the people Anesh sent because if they're not, we're in deep trouble.

"What are your names?" the woman asks.

"I'm Lylon Porter, and this is Valerie Ray. The dog's name is Rudy," I reply over my shoulder.

While I can't see who they are, I know there are at least three of them. There were three gun clicks, and I doubt one person holds three guns. I feel a little better after they asked our names because the Thorn are not the name-asking types. Anesh must have described us, but still, being held at gunpoint unsettles me.

"You can turn around now," the woman says.

Slowly, I turn around and see three people dressed in police uniforms holstering their guns. The woman in the center is clearly in charge, while the two men with her seem able to hold themselves in a fight. I recognize the tall man on her right. He's the school's on-site police officer.

"Sorry about that. We needed to make sure we got the right people. I'm Chief of Police Linda Barman, and these are officers Winston Pax and Mason Gray."

"Good to meet you," Valerie and I reply in unison.

Chief Barman takes off the walkie-talkie from her belt and notifies the others that they've got us. She then looks back at us.

"Alright, we need to get going. Gray, cover our rear, and Pax keep your eyes open," Chief Barman says as we start moving down the street.

We walk along the fence of the park. The direction we're going is familiar, so I hurry as fast as my limp allows near Chief Barman.

"Chief Barman, are you taking us to the school?" I ask.

"Linda is fine. And what makes you think we're going to the school?"

"Well, officer Gray is the on-site police officer at the school, and this is the same route I take to school."

"Anesh told me you're smart. Yes, we're going to the school."

"So, you have a group there?"

"Yeah. About fifty people. The school has enough space and food for weeks, maybe even months."

"Are you the group leader?"

"Kid, do you always ask this many questions?"

"Sorry. No, just curious," I say and decide to stop questioning her.

"No, I'm not the leader," Linda eventually responds. "I'm barely fit to oversee two police officers, let alone two kids."

"If you're Chief of Police, I'm sure you're more than qualified to lead a small group."

She flashes a small smile that quickly fades into a frown. "You have no idea."

"So, then who's in charge?"

"You'll see."

I fall back in line with Valerie so I don't annoy Chief Barman. Rudy is back to his happy self, his tongue hanging out with his tail wagging as we walk. Valerie puts her hand in mine, and we continue to walk down the sidewalk.

"Did you get all your questions answered?"

"Not all, but most. We're going to the school," I say.

Valerie smirks. "You were four feet in front of me. I heard."

After ten minutes of walking, the school building comes into view. This is the last place I expected to return to. But I'm happy to be part of a group, as there's safety in numbers. We make it to the parking lot when Chief Barman takes off her walkie-talkie.

"We're back. Open the gate. Over."

"Copy that. Over," a man on the other end replies.

All the lights are off, giving it a creepy vibe. Even at night, the school usually has some lights on, but not tonight. The school's yellow bricks and blacked-out windows make it look like a prison cell block. We make it to the front entrance and the door swings open. Two more officers in uniform emerge and ask if we have any weapons on us. I hand over the gun, happy to get my father's murder weapon off my hands. They let us keep our pocketknives and then give Rudy a treat.

Once inside, the officers close and lock the front doors behind us. One of them stays to keep watch while the rest of us follow Chief Barman farther into the school.

"We only have a few rules. Don't yell, don't turn the lights on in exterior rooms, and respect everyone else. We're trying to do what we can to keep everyone alive. Food is served at the cafeteria, and almost everyone sleeps in the gym. We have sleeping bags for you to use."

"Thank you. We really appreciate it," Valerie says.

"Now you can find out who runs the place. He wants to see you," Linda says outside the principal's office.

The office previously occupied by the wide Mr. Girlin is now accommodating a short Asian man I know very well. Mr. Liu is our Mayor, and over the years, he's attended many of our school events. His daughter, Hannah, is a grade below us.

Mr. Liu greets us with a smile and gestures for us to sit.

"It's nice to meet you both. Lylon and Valerie, is it?" Mr. Liu asks.

"Yes, sir. And Rudy," I say, nodding at Rudy, who's sitting next to me with his head in my lap.

"Ah. Can't forget Rudy. Anesh told me that you're both good friends of his, and he didn't want to leave you out there."

"Yes, sir. Anesh has been my best friend since first grade."

"Good, good. I'm sure you're both exhausted, so I'll make this short. Did Chief Barman explain the rules?" Mr. Liu asks.

"Yes, sir, she did," Valerie replies.

"Good. If you need light, use candles. We have some in the gym that you can carry around with you. Although we would prefer it if you stayed with the group. Most people here stay in the gym, but we've offered each family a classroom to stay in. All the classrooms surrounding the gym are available, but only a few families are using them. If you like, I can arrange a room for each of you."

"That'd be great, but we only need one room. We're not picky," Valerie says and glances at me.

"Yeah, only one will do," I confirm.

"Okay. That saves another room in case another family shows up. You can take B110. It's right across the hall from the gym. Some officers walk up and down the halls with walkies all night, so we're secure. The basketball locker rooms are available for showering, which I assume you would like to use, Lylon?"

"Yes, sir. I need to get this crap off me."

"How did you get that much blood all over you?" he asks with a frown.

"I'd rather not talk about it."

Mr. Liu studies me for a moment before speaking again. "Alright. After you clean up, you can go to the cafeteria for a hot meal. We have all sorts of stuff in there, and one of the parents has volunteered to cook. We already ate dinner, but you can heat up some of the leftovers in the main fridge."

"Thank you. You have no idea how much this means to us," I say.

"Yeah, no problem. I'm sure you're familiar with the school's layout, but of course, you can ask us if you need anything."

"Yes sir. Thanks again," I say as Valerie and I stand.

Valerie and I leave the office with Rudy following and head to the gym in the middle of the hall on the right. On the left is B110. Our room. Since it's an interior room, we can use the lights. I flip the switch on, and I almost squeal with joy. Standing in the middle of the floor is none other than Anesh.

"Dude! You almost gave me a heart attack!" I say and rush to him for a hug.

It feels good to see him again. Soon Valerie joins in on the hug, and we stay embraced for a little while.

"Man, y'all reek," he says with a smile as he pulls away.

"It's good to see you too," I say.

"What happened to you two?"

"You have no idea," Valerie says.

Rudy jumps up on Anesh and starts to lick his face, and that brings a smile to my face.

"And who's this?" he asks.

"He's Rudy. Lylon's dad found him."

"How'd you know we would be in this room?" I ask.

"I wasn't sure, but they told me they'd offer this room and the next to you. I kinda figured that you'd share a room. So what happened to your dad?" he asks, still petting Rudy.

"Look…uh… I really need a shower. We can catch up later at the cafeteria. Can you meet us there?"

"Sure. I'll give you time to settle in," Anesh says and starts for the door.

Once he leaves, I open my bag and grab a change of clothes. Valerie pours the rest of the dog food into a pile on the floor, which Rudy immediately begins to devour.

"I'll be back in a bit," I say to Valerie and leave for a much-needed shower.

Everywhere I look in the gym, there are sleeping bags. I see about thirty people in here, but there are way more sleeping bags. The only lighting comes from candles, and I stumble my way to the guys' locker room.

The showers are empty, and I sigh in relief. I set my clothes on a bench and start to strip down. The showers are just an open area with showerheads mounted to the walls. I bet the girls' locker room has actual stalls, but I'm not complaining. I just need to get all the blood off me.

The tiles are cold against my feet, but the water is pleasantly warm when I turn on the showerhead. Putting my hands against the wall, I close my eyes and let the water slide down my back. I don't have soap with me, so I do the best I can. Soon the water beneath my feet turns red.

I close my eyes, and images of everything that happened today filter into my mind. No matter how hard I try for my mind to go blank, I don't succeed. I wish there was a way to get the orb back, or to at least have used it when I had the chance. But most of all, I wish I had my parents with me. I hope the officers here can keep us safe, but something tells me we're running on borrowed time.

The door to the locker room opens, and I close my eyes, enjoying the last few seconds of solitude I'm left.

"Can I join you?" Valerie asks from behind me. Surprised, I go to turn my head, but Valerie's voice stops me. "No peeking, pervert."

"I'm the pervert? You're the one who's in the guys' locker room."

"Details, details," she says with a chuckle. Her soft fingers trace my naked back, and I shiver from the sensation. "I brought soap. I also locked the door, so we won't be disturbed."

Her touch is like a balm to my tortured soul, and I close my eyes, reveling in the sensation. This is exactly what I need right now.

"I feel like a failure," I say.

"You're no failure."

"Really? Because I had the orb and lost it, Charlie and Dave got killed right in front of me, and Dad got shot when I was with him."

"And yet none of it was your fault. Just like it wasn't my fault that my parents died in a car accident."

Shaking my head, I feel like the worst person in the world. I haven't been there for her; not like she has for me. I keep talking about how bad I have it, but I never asked Valerie how she's coping with all that has happened to her.

"I've been a horrible boyfriend."

"I didn't say that. Don't be so hard on yourself. This is the first time we've lost someone and under such circumstances. We hardly know how to feel, let alone react."

"I'm so sorry."

Her kind words make me feel even more guilty. I've been too overcome with my own grief to even ask her how she feels.

"It's fine. We both lost people we love. The only thing we can do now is to stick together and be there for each other."

Valerie comes to me and puts her head on the crook of my neck. Instinctively, I close my eyes and allow myself the luxury of picturing life after the invasion. We'll be finally free to be together and start a family of our own. My dreams disperse suddenly when Valerie pulls away and starts to wash herself behind me. I'm tempted to turn around, but I only manage to tilt my head slightly before Valerie notices.

"I said no peeking."

"And I say this isn't fair. You get to see me butt naked, but I can't see you?"

"Oh, it's totally fair," she says with a small giggle.

I hear Valerie walking away, and I'm a little miffed when she doesn't return. I spend a few moments under the showerhead, and when I turn it off, I stay here dripping with water. Immediately, I miss the warmth of the water, and as I'm about to leave, I hear Valerie's voice again.

"You have my permission to turn around now," she says.

I glance over my shoulder and see her in her underwear getting dressed.

"How did you dry yourself?" I ask.

"I used the paper towels mostly," she says, nodding at the other side of the locker room.

I use half of the giant paper roll to dry my body, and as I'm drying my hair with the hairdryer, I hear a bang at the door.

"What was that?" Valerie calls from across the room.

"Someone's at the door," I say and walk back to get dressed.

I throw my bloodied dirty clothes in the trash. Even though I could just wash them, I don't want any reminders of this awful day.

Taking Valerie's hand, we head to the door, half-expecting to find ten people waiting outside. Thankfully, it's only Anesh, looking worried.

"You good, man? You've been in there almost an hour, and I can't find Valerie."

"We're good," I say with a faint smile.

"I'm right here," Valerie says as she opens the door all the way. Anesh's eyes grow wide at the realization that we've been together in the guys' locker room.

"Did y'all—" he starts.

"No," we both say at the same time, then laugh.

"Okay… Uh… Let's uh… let's go grab something to eat."

We walk out of the gym and stop by our room so Valerie can drop off her clothes. Rudy has finally gone to sleep on top of a blanket Anesh brought along with two sleeping bags for us. He must have cleared out some of the desks, too, because we have more room now.

Most people are fast asleep as we head to the cafeteria, so we try to be as quiet as possible.

"Let's see," Anesh says, opening the fridge. "Either school meatloaf or popcorn chicken."

"Popcorn chicken!" Valerie and I both say.

"Figured as much," Anesh says and pulls out a big bowl.

We eat it in silence, and Anesh stares at us, bemused. We must look like we haven't eaten in years. At least that's what it feels like.

Once we finish eating, Anesh learns for the first time the full unabridged version of what has happened to Valerie and me since yesterday. While it's good to talk and get it off our chest, he seems shocked.

"Man… that's a load of crap. I'm so sorry," Anesh says.

"Yeah, it's been tough," Valerie responds.

"When you told me about your dad, I never imagined he died like that. I hope I didn't say anything to upset you."

"No, don't worry," I say.

"So, you really had an orb?" he asks.

"Yeah… and I let it slip away. So, what happened to you?" I ask in dire need of changing the subject.

"Not as much as you guys, but my mom she… uh… she didn't make it," he says as he looks away. He obviously didn't want to talk about it.

Tears well in my eyes that my best friend lost yet another parent so tragically. We're all left without our parents, and it's not right. We now have to figure out how to navigate this invasion without them. Thankfully we have the police to look after us now.

"I left the walkie at home in case one of you came to my house. Chief Barman lives across the street, and she brought me here. That's pretty much it," Anesh finishes.

"So, what's the deal with Chief Barman? She seemed off when we met her. Said she wasn't fit to be Chief of Police," I say.

Anesh frowns. "I overheard her and the mayor yesterday. A Thorn got ahold of her four-year-old. She tried to shoot him, but our weapons can't kill or harm them. They murdered her kid in front of her, took the body, and let her live."

"Why, though?" Valerie asks.

Anesh shrugs. "Who knows? Nothing these monsters do makes sense."

We sit there in silence for a couple of minutes, and I have to stifle a yawn.

"I'm sorry," I say. "I think tiredness is getting the best of me."

"Don't worry, we've got plenty of time to catch up," he says.

"You're right, Anesh," Valerie says. "We'll talk more tomorrow."

After we say our goodnights and Anesh leaves, Valerie and I clean the kitchen in silence. I keep thinking about the Thorn, and the possibility of them being here to test us. What would this test be though? And when would it happen?

"Ready?" Valerie asks, wiping her hands with a towel after she cleans the last plate.

"Go ahead. I want to talk to Mr. Liu to get his thoughts on my theory about the Thorn being here to test us. I just can't get it out of my mind."

"Okay," she says, "That's probably a good idea. I'll meet you back at the room." She gives me a quick kiss on the cheek and exits the kitchen.

I make my way to the principal's office and knock on the door.

"Come in," Mr. Liu says, and I open the door.

Our Mayor looks exhausted and disheveled, with dark circles under his eyes.

"You look like you could use some sleep," I say.

"Yes. That would be nice. What can I do for you, Lylon?"

"I have a theory, and I'd like to run it by you if you have some time."

"Of course. Please take a seat."

"I think the Thorn aren't here for just our resources. If my theory is right, then this is a test of some kind. They gave us orbs, and the leader said it would be interesting to watch us fight each other for them. That's a strange thing to say in his first message to us. It'd only make sense if they're actually here to observe us."

Mr. Liu scratches his chin deep in thought. "It's an interesting theory, and you might be right, but I can't see what we can do about it."

"I don't know. Perhaps we need to do our best to pass this test. We have no idea what it is, but it's there. I'm sure of it. We'd better keep an eye out for it," I say.

"Perhaps you're right, but right now, our main focus is to stay alive, and I think we're doing a good job of it."

"But, sir, if we fail this test—"

"Lylon, please. I'm tired, and I want to see my wife and daughter. Can we talk about this tomorrow?"

I sigh. "Yes, sir."

"Alright. Go get some rest," he says.

"Night," I say and leave the office once more.

Shaking my head, I walk down the hallway to our room. Maybe Mr. Liu doesn't believe me, but Valerie does, which is all that matters.

I get to the room and crack the door open. The only light in the room is coming from a candle next to Valerie's sleeping bag. Rudy is still sound asleep on the blanket next to her. Closing the door, I strip down to my underwear and climb into my sleeping bag next to Valerie's. I blow out the candle and put my head down. The floor has a carpet, but it's still hard on my back. Valerie moves a little closer to me, and our heads touch.

"What did he say?" she asks.

"He doesn't believe me. He didn't say it, but I can tell."

"Well, it doesn't matter. He doesn't know you like I do. You're smart, and I'd believe you over anyone else any time of the day."

"Thanks," I say with a chuckle.

"Goodnight, Lylon. I love you."

"I love you too, Valerie. So, so, much," I say and close my eyes.

Chapter Twenty

Day Three

Something wets my face, and I reluctantly open my eyes to find Rudy licking me. Scratching my new friend behind his ears, I sit up and wonder what time it is. I can barely make out Valerie's silhouette, still asleep next to me, so it must be pretty early. I feel groggy, and I wish I could sleep more. Surprisingly, the moment my head hit the floor last night, I fell asleep. It was a dreamless sleep, and I'm grateful because I don't think I could have handled another nightmare.

Crouching next to Valerie, I pick up the candle and a box of matches. I strike one of them, and the flame warms my fingers as I use it to light the candle. The clock next to the door reads 6:03 a.m. It really doesn't feel like I've slept for seven hours, but it never does in the morning.

I almost open the door to walk out, but then remember I need to get dressed. Other than my underwear, the only thing I have on is my knee brace. It reeks since I've only taken it off to shower, but it's all I've got, and I need to keep it on. I throw on the same clothes from yesterday and walk out the door with Rudy hot on my heels.

The first thing that registers once I'm in the hallway is the smell of fresh bacon. My stomach growls, making me realize how hungry I am.

I open the door to the gym, and Anesh comes to me. Despite the low light, I can see he's tired. His short black hair is sticking up, and he's squinting even though it's dark. He has pajama pants and a plain gray t-shirt on and covers his mouth to hide a yawn.

"I was just about to wake you up," he says in a low voice.

"Well, Rudy beat you to it."

"Is Valerie up too?" he asks.

"No. Still sound asleep," I say.

"You might want to wake her up. They just started making breakfast, and if we go now, it'll still be fresh."

"Alright, I'll wake her," I say and return to our room.

I feel a little bad that I won't let her sleep some more. I set the candle next to her and take a moment to watch her sleep. She's so beautiful that I'm tempted to lie down next to her, but Anesh is right, we need to eat. I shake her shoulder gently, and she groans.

"What time is it?" she asks.

"6:15. They're making breakfast, and Anesh said we should go now while it's fresh."

"Ugh. Okay. I'm coming," she says and sits up.

To my astonishment, Valerie doesn't have any clothes on, so I turn the other way to give her some privacy. When she's fully dressed, she walks over and hugs me. I kiss her and take her hand to lead her to the kitchen.

"How'd you sleep?" I ask as we walk down the hall toward the cafeteria. Rudy is walking beside us, and I hope they have some extra food because we ran out of dog food last night.

"Not bad. It was a little hard on my back, and my neck is sore, but other than that, I was able to sleep through the whole night. What about you?"

"I've slept better, but also worse. I wish we had actual pillows other than just the sleeping bag's basic support, but I can't complain."

We enter the cafeteria and find Anesh at one of the round tables near the food line. He has a plate in front of him, but all that's left are crumbs. It smells even better in here, which makes me even more hungry. Rudy seems to like the smell, too, as he starts licking his chops.

"There's bacon, eggs, and hash browns in the line. Get a plate for Rudy as well if you want," Anesh says as we approach.

I grab two plates and start piling on food. Usually, I would eat a lot more, but I know other families will wake up soon, so I don't take a lot. For the same reason, I don't give Rudy too much, but also because I'm not sure this type of food is good for him. We leave the line and join Anesh. Rudy busies himself with his food the moment I put his plate on the floor.

"Who cooked all this?" I ask Anesh.

"Mr. Hanson. He volunteered to cook meals. And by cook, I mean take all the frozen processed crap out of the school freezers and heat it up. He's basically a lunch lady."

I chuckle. "Lunch lady."

"I'm serious. You should see him. The guy has man boobs," Anesh says, and we both laugh at that. Valerie doesn't seem to appreciate the joke, though.

"Don't you think that's a little rude?" she asks with her eyebrow raised.

"Sorry," I say, falling silent.

"Okay, it was a little funny," Valerie says after a moment.

We resume eating, and I'm surprised at how good it tastes. Come to think of it, last night's meal wasn't bad either, but this tastes like a home-cooked breakfast. Just like Mom used to make. The bacon is crispy and has a sweet, smoky flavor, and the eggs are surprisingly good for school food. They have cheese and pepper on them, mixed with diced tomatoes. Once I finish eating, I sit back in my chair and relax.

"That was not too bad for school food," I say.

Anesh nods. "Yeah. Mr. Hanson is actually a pretty good cook."

"The bacon is my favorite," Valerie says.

"Mine too," Anesh and I both agree.

"So, what's our plan for after this?" Anesh asks.

"We don't really have one right now. We're just focusing on staying alive at the moment," I say.

"Why? Do you have a plan?" Valerie asks.

"Actually, I was thinking about hiking Everest," he says.

"Mount Everest?" Valerie chuckles.

"Yeah. What's wrong with that?"

"Nothing's wrong with that, but how are you gonna get there, dude?" I ask.

"Uh, by plane. How else?"

"Dude, do you really think that planes will be in the air after the Thorn leave?"

"I mean, I don't know. You don't need to rain on my parade, though."

"I'm not. I think it'd be cool to hike Everest. But good luck getting there."

"I'll get there. You'll see," he says with a determined gleam in his eyes.

"I guess we will."

The other families start to file into the cafeteria as we continue to talk about various things. Things we would normally talk about on a normal school day. We pretend it's a normal school day with its usual problems. I say how I have too much AP Calculus homework and that Mr. Huy was even more boring than yesterday. Valerie then says that her English class is a piece of cake, and everyone in there needs to learn how to turn stuff in. Then Anesh complains about how he got sent to Mr. Girlin's office for calling his history teacher a dingbat, which caused us all to laugh. We all wish so badly for this to go back to normal.

Even though almost everyone staying at the school is in the cafeteria now, it still feels dead. I spot Hannah Liu, the mayor's daughter, heading toward us. She looks well-rested with her straight black hair and pale skin. We all smile at her as she stops at our table and pulls out a chair.

"Hey, Hannah," Valerie says.

"Hi, guys."

"Hello," Anesh and I reply.

We never talked to her much, but I'm glad to see another familiar face.

"Hannah, do you know if your dad has been in contact with another group of people?" Valerie asks.

"Yes, he has. There's another group on the outskirts of Dallas, although we don't know exactly where. We've been in contact with them over high-powered police walkie-talkies," Hannah says. "Why do you ask?"

"I knew it!" Valerie says. "Because I was with them yesterday, and they were in contact with another group. I remembered when we got here, but it was late and I just wanted to sleep. Carly is there, and her mom is leading them. There are about thirty people staying in a hotel."

"Hmm. Thanks for the info. I'll let my dad know. Are they safe?"

"They are as safe as they can be, taking the same precautions as you do here. They have their windows covered, don't use lights, and keep their voices down. From what I saw, their area has been untouched. The street down from them, though, is in shambles. Honestly though, how safe can we really be?" Valerie asks.

"We're very safe! My dad keeps us safe, so we won't have to worry about the Thorn getting to us. They don't know we're here," Hannah says proudly.

As much as I want to believe her, I can't. It's total crap.

"Hannah, you do realize the Thorn can cloak themselves, right?" I ask.

"Of course. Who doesn't know that by now?"

"Well, if they are cloaked, they could be watching us right now, and we wouldn't even know it. So, tell me, how can we possibly be sure we're safe here?" I ask her.

She opens her mouth to respond but then closes it again.

"Hannah, your dad can't protect us from everything," Anesh says.

"We need to be prepared for everything," I add.

"I know that, but don't you think the Thorn would've already come here if they knew about us?"

"Honestly, no. We have no idea of their plans or tactics. For all we know, they want us to get together so it'd be easier for them to execute us."

As soon as I finish my sentence, Rudy lifts his head, his ears shooting up. He frantically walks back and forth between Valerie and me with an ear-piercing whine.

"What is it Rudy?" I ask him. He looks at me with wide eyes, which confirms my theory from earlier. He can smell the Thorn.

The cafeteria erupts with screams as Thorn after Thorn appear out of thin air surrounding the entire group. The whole community starts shielding their faces as the Thorn draw their cannons and take aim. Children start bawling, their parents putting themselves between them and the ruthless murderers.

But the cannons never go off. One Thorn soldier steps forward. He looks the same as the rest, ginormous and hideous, but with some kind of alien war medal on his shoulder. He must rank higher than regular soldiers but under the leader.

He speaks in a deep, gravelly voice. "We are not here to kill you. If you follow directions, that is. We're taking you downtown, where you'll receive further instruction. Either follow or die."

Chapter Twenty-One

7:30 AM

The Thorn put us into a line to leave the building. If I've counted right, there are twenty-two soldiers and the general in charge. I'm between Valerie and Anesh while Rudy growls next to me. We're waiting for the Thorn to search the rest of the school for others. I know that all of us are here, but let the soldiers keep searching so there'll be fewer of them here to deal with. Valerie is at the front of the line, and the soldier watching our section is pacing back and forth. I turn slightly and whisper so only Valerie and Anesh can both hear me.

"He takes ten seconds to go from here to there. Once his back is to us, we have a shot."

"You think I haven't figured that out yet?" Anesh whispers back.

"Take the first right, and we'll go from there," Valerie says.

I would be lying if I said I'm surprised we're all on the same page. We've known each other long enough to figure out what we're all thinking, but still, Valerie joining us is unexpected, considering she is a stickler for rules. I guess when giant aliens are invading our planet, it's okay to break them.

The soldier is now facing us, coming our way, his massive feet making vibrations with every step. Closer and closer. Step after step. Finally, he reaches us, but instead of turning back around, he stops and stares. His eyes aren't directed at us but at Rudy. A slight grin comes to his hideous face, and he licks his lips as his dark eyes continue to stare at my dog.

Rudy starts to growl, and I have to grab his collar to make sure he doesn't attack. I'm disgusted that this beast would even think about eating a pet. But then again, I'm disgusted with everything the Thorn are doing. Finally, he turns and walks the other way. Now is our chance.

"Now!" I whisper.

Valerie takes off, and we all follow her. I look over my shoulder as the soldier is about to turn back around. We need to run faster. We take the first right like Valerie said and scamper down the dimly lit hallway. I have no idea where we're going, but we need to get out of here.

"Where are we going?" Anesh calls out from behind me, panting.

"The nearest exit," Valerie says. "But we don't know where the Thorn searching the hallways are."

We take a few more turns, and the exit comes into view at the end of the hallway. We're all running as fast as we can. My knee is burning with pain, but I push through it and run even faster. We're halfway down the hall when a Thorn soldier comes around the opposite corner, blocking our path. We skid to a stop, but Rudy's nails make him slide right at the Thorn. Rudy yelps in pain as the Thorn kicks him with more force than necessary, sending my poor dog crashing into a locker.

"No!" I cry, rushing toward Rudy.

I only make it two steps before another Thorn soldier appears in front of me and slaps me hard across the face with his ginormous hand. My face flares up, and I double over in excruciating pain. I kneel on the ground, clutching my face.

A small hand touches my shoulder, and when I look up, Valerie is bent over, trying to help me up. She mouths something, but I'm too stunned to decode sounds into speech.

"You're not going anywhere, boy," the soldier who hit me says.

I look up to find four more soldiers on us with their cannons drawn. One of them shoves me forward, back down the hallway toward the cafeteria. I chance a look over my shoulder and see Rudy, lifeless and mangled, on the floor. What have I done? This is all my fault. If we hadn't tried to run, Rudy would still be alive. I force back tears. All Rudy did was try to protect us. We just met him, yet I feel like he's been in my life for years. Why did they have to take away my dog too?

We make it back to the cafeteria, and the general is glaring at the remaining humans. Everyone seems to know that we wouldn't get far. We're forced back in line, and the general comes our way. I'm expecting him to prove a point by killing one of us, and I brace myself.

"If you try to run again, I'll kill you myself. And I'll make sure it's more painful than you can ever imagine," he says with a grin.

The rest of the soldiers make it back to the cafeteria and halt in front of the general.

"That's the last of them," one of them says.

"Good. Time to get moving," the general says and motions for our line to move.

***

The Thorn lead us down the side of the highway in a single file line like prisoners. That's because we essentially are prisoners to them. It's very cold this morning, and we can just make out the massive warship's outline through the clouds. There's a slight mist, and I shiver since all I have on are jeans and a long-sleeved shirt. Now I regret throwing out my bloody hoodie because no matter how dirty it was, it would've kept me warm. My face still stings from where the soldier smacked me, and my knee feels even worse from all the running and walking.

Valerie is still right in front of me with Anesh behind me, but now there's no more Rudy. I can't get the image of his lifeless body out of my head. The way his head was bent back and his ribcage looked crushed. I wish we hadn't run. He would still be here if we hadn't. It was my idea to run, and that got him killed. I just hope the Thorn don't mess with his body.

As we approach the town square, I notice a crowd of people, and when we join them, I estimate we're a little over one hundred. On the wooden stage, where live performances are usually held, stand many Thorn soldiers. But one of them is not like the rest. He's much taller and bigger than the rest—even the general. His arms and legs are twice the size of a normal Thorn soldier, and he's wearing a massive medallion around his thick neck.

He's the Thorn leader I saw on TV.

Whispers erupt among the crowd, and I see Valerie's friend Carly up ahead. The Thorn must have found their group as well. We join the group at the back, and the soldiers form a wall behind us, all the way around the entire crowd. I grab Valerie's wrist and pull her close to me. I don't trust anything or anyone down here but Valerie and Anesh.

"What do you think we are doing down here?" I ask.

"I have no idea. You don't think they'll execute us, right?" Valerie asks.

I want to tell her no, but I don't want to lie to her. But why would the leader of the Thorn need to be here for that? Something is about to happen.

Anesh comes closer. "Thinking about running again?"

"It's crossed my mind. Are you in?"

"Yup!"

"I count forty-five soldiers, the general, and the leader. If we can sneak out the back of the crowd, we should be safe," I say.

"There aren't many guards behind us. It might work," Valerie says.

Anesh lowers his head to avoid the stare of a Thorn soldier. "Maybe we should find out why we're down here first before we try to run."

"Whatever it is, it can't be good," I say.

The leader of the Thorn takes a step forward and stands tall before us. The wooden stage whines and creaks under him as if it's about to give way at any second. He scans the crowd, and for a moment, his stare is directed at me. The grin he gives me sends shivers down my spine. He doesn't need to speak loud for everyone to hear, but his voice is deeper than all the other Thorn soldiers I've heard.

"People of Dallas. You might be wondering why you're all down here. First, I want you to look around you. There might be people you know, and there might be people you have never seen before. Either way, everyone here is your competitor. All that stands here now are the remaining humans in Dallas. And now is your chance to earn something. I'm here to offer something that will aid you—"

"We ain't wantin' what you got!" a man with a southern accent calls out from the crowd.

"How can we trust you after you've taken everything from us?" a woman shouts.

"That's it! I've had enough of these lies!" another man yells and steps forward, drawing his pistol.

With practiced efficiency, the man fires his gun and the bullet finds its aim at the leader's big forehead. For a normal human, death would be instantaneous, but on the Thorn leader, it just bounces and falls down. The crowd goes silent as the leader picks up the bullet. He holds it in his hand before he crushes it between two fingers and tosses it into the crowd.

"That was a big mistake. I was going to offer you a chance at something. An offer not one of you could refuse."

The leader holds out his hand and an orb appears out of thin air, floating above his palm. This orb glows brighter than the one I found, but it has the same green color. I want to run up there and grab it, but I fight back the temptation.

"I was going to have you all compete for this. It would have been your chance for another orb. Clearly, you don't care for a second chance to bring a loved one back."

"We don't want to fight for your pleasure!" the man with the gun screams.

"Hmm… Fine. Have it your way," the leader says as he flicks his wrist towards us, starting the bloodbath.

Chapter Twenty-Two

10:30 AM

All we can do is watch in horror as the Thorn soldiers draw their cannons and fire. The people on the outer part of the group fall down, screaming in pain as their flesh begins to boil.

Their cannons must need some time to recharge because many soldiers come forward and begin to brutally beat the remaining humans. I already knew how ruthless they are, but this is much worse. It doesn't matter how old or big anyone here is, the Thorn don't hold back. One soldier smashes his fist into a child's head so hard it comes off, blood spraying everywhere as it rolls to the ground. Another man is kicked down, and his skull is smashed so hard his brain matter is visible.

I'm looking at death straight in the face.

The Thorn are too big and too strong to take alone, but somehow a group of people renders one soldier immobile. Two people are clutching each leg, and one person is on his back. Two other Thorn soldiers try to shoot the humans off, but one of them misses and hits the Thorn instead. For the first time, we see what it's like when a Thorn is shot with one of their own weapons. His thick grey skin starts to explode off his body, but the soldier doesn't cry out in pain. He's completely silent as his skin melts and his whole body becomes a grey oily liquid on the ground. The only thing left is bones and his armor when he's finally dead.

I glance around and see several people I know on the ground. Carly, Mr. Liu, Hannah, and many others are dead. The human number wanes fast, and we're sure to be next. Then I see the man with the pistol as he draws it once more and takes aim. Before he gets a chance to fire it, a soldier grabs his arm and forces it all the way around. The man screams as his shoulder is ripped from its socket, and in his twitching, the gun goes off.

Horrified, I look at the end of the barrel, and a moment later, something swishes past my ear. But it doesn't hit me. Gargling sounds come from behind me, and I turn to find my best friend clutching his throat as blood gushes down his white shirt.

"Anesh!" I yell and try to go to him, but something pulls me back.

I look over my shoulder and find Valerie tugging at my shirt.

"We need to go, now!" she shouts over the loud screams of pain.

Without taking my eyes from Anesh, I take tentative steps backward. Another person I care about is dying in front of my eyes, and there's nothing I can do. He'll never travel the world or hike Everest like he wanted. My first friend, best friend, part of my family. I watch his chest as it rises and falls rapidly. Until it slows and life leaves his body. All in a matter of seconds.

I look away and take off with Valerie. All the guards at the back have moved around the sides to beat people, so our chances are good. If we manage to sneak into an alley, they might lose us.

We bolt to an alley with brick on each side. It's narrow, but Valerie and I are still able to run next to each other. It would only fit one Thorn soldier at a time, which makes me feel a little confident about our odds. Valerie tries all the back doors and finally finds one unlocked and yanks it open.

"In here," she says.

We rush inside and close the door as quietly as we can. It's somewhat dark, but I can make out Valerie's outline. We wait for a few minutes in silence and listen for signs of anyone following us. Time passes as we wait impatiently, but nothing happens.

"I think they lost us," Valerie whispers.

"Lost us? They didn't even follow us. They must have seen us run, but they didn't follow," I say with disbelief.

"Maybe they didn't see us, or maybe they were too busy with everyone else."

"I don't think so. There's no way they didn't. And there were plenty of them. Why would they let us go?" I respond, forcing back tears.

I pull Valerie into a hug. I don't know what to do. All I want is for my parents, Anesh, Valerie's parents, Rudy, and all the people I knew my entire life to be alive. The Thorn have taken it all away from me, and I want it back, but I won't focus on what's already gone. Valerie is all I have left, and I won't let them take her too.

"Anesh… he…"

"He's gone. Just gone," I say.

"That bullet could have hit any one of us."

"Yet it hit Anesh," I respond.

"Yeah, but we won't let him die in vain."

"How can we avenge him. They're too strong for us."

"There are other ways," she says and tightens her hold of my hand.

"How?"

"We survive. We survive for him, our parents, friends. For everyone. We keep fighting, and we keep surviving until they leave."

"How can you be so sure we'll make it? It's all about luck," I say bitterly.

"Maybe not. We're still here, right? Any chance we could have been taken or killed; we were not. We will survive this. I know it."

Somehow it makes me feel better, and I start to have confidence that we'll survive. What Valerie says about us still being alive is true. There have been countless instances where we could've died, yet we were spared. Maybe we're meant to survive this somehow. Either way, we need to get out of here.

"What now?" I ask.

"Now we run. And we don't stop until we're safe."

Chapter Twenty-Three

10:50 AM

The door whines as Valerie opens it slowly, allowing a small amount of light to creep in. I peek outside and look left and right to make sure no one has followed us.

There's nothing there, but that doesn't mean the Thorn aren't following. I have an idea. Just because the Thorn can turn invisible doesn't mean they can't be touched. I walk into the alley, pick up a rock, and throw it behind us. It flies through the air and doesn't hit anything until it hits the ground. Nothing behind us. I do the same thing, only this time I throw the rock in front. Nothing again. With the coast clear, we continue ahead.

The alley leads to a much wider back street with fire escape stairs on each side. It's a small apartment complex that probably costs more than it's worth. We turn left and walk down the wider alley until it ends up on the road running in front of the building.

"Where are we going?" Valerie asks.

"I thought you knew."

I hope we can get far away from here, but I have no idea where to go. I look at Valerie, and she squints her eyes, a sign that she's thinking hard.

"We can head down that street and exit into the neighborhood over there. Maybe we can find someone who can help," she says, pointing two streets down.

"Valerie, you heard what the leader said. That one hundred something people were all that were left in Dallas…We're it."

"But we might not be. Come on."

Valerie hurries into the street, and I follow. Of course, the leader could be lying, but I don't think so. He's keeping something from us, that's for sure, but I don't think it's the remaining population in Dallas. I'm in the city center, yet it feels like I'm in a ghost town, walking around abandoned houses and eerily quiet neighborhoods. I honestly think we're it.

I still feel like the Thorn are here to test us. I just haven't figured out how or why. A chilling thought crosses my mind. What if they never leave? What if they bring other Thorn here to inhabit the Earth? What if they just kill off the rest of us, making us think there's still hope when there is none? But then why would they take prisoners? That can't be it then. Whatever the test is, though, it can't be anything good.

We make it to the next street, and my knee starts to flare up. All the running finally gets to me, but I refuse to stop. We pick up the pace until we're practically jogging as we round corner after corner. This street has so many cars piled up, there had to have been a major accident. There's also dried blood on the ground and a shoe with a foot still in it. I shiver at the sight. We look away as we pass by the wreck and continue until the neighborhood comes into view.

"We just need to get out of downtown," Valerie says.

"I agree. Once we're out of the city center, we should be safer. The neighborhood should give us more places we could hide as well," I say.

We cross the street and enter the small neighborhood Valerie was talking about. Something about it seems familiar, but I can't put my finger on what. Maybe it's the freshly cut grass or the two trees in front of every house. Or maybe it's the way every house looks the same, or how there's a small park in the center of the neighborhood. Whatever it is, I can't put my finger on it.

Halfway down the street, I stop and lean against a truck parked in front of a two-story house. My knee is killing me, and I need to rest for a moment. Valerie notices me and walks back to me.

"You okay?" she asks.

"Yeah, it's my knee. I just need a moment."

"If you need, I can help support your weight."

"I should be good in a couple of minutes."

It would actually be nice to have her help, but it would slow us down when we need to get away as soon as possible. I stretch my leg out, but it gets worse, so I stop. Instead, I stand on my right leg and let my left dangle, not putting any weight on it. I stay like this for a couple of minutes until I decide we need to continue.

"Ready?" Valerie asks.

"Yeah. I'm good," I say, forcing myself forward.

But we don't make it far. A gunshot is heard in the distance, and we both stop to look around. The shot was close, possibly the next street over. Too close. I start to walk forward again.

"Ly—" Valerie wheezes.

Something in her voice makes my heart stop. Slowly, I turn around and meet her wide eyes as she clutches her stomach. Blood seeps through. Her dark blue shirt turns an even darker shade as the blood soaks through it.

That's when I see him.

In the distance, a man is holding a rifle. As soon as our eyes meet, he bolts down the street. My first instinct is to chase after him, to kill him with my bare hands. But Valerie falls into my arms before I get a chance to move.

"No, no, not you too!" I cry, landing on my butt with Valerie's head in my lap.

In an effort to do something—anything—to help her, I pull up her shirt, frantic to save her. Maybe if I apply pressure to the wound, I'll stop the bleeding until I can get someone to help. She grabs my hands, forcing me to stop.

"Valerie! What happened to us surviving?" I sob, tears streaming down my face.

Valerie puts one hand on the side of my face, the other still on her stomach. She can't speak, only piercing me with her green eyes. Her dying eyes. Tears trickle down her face, and every breath she takes is a struggle. I know she doesn't have long.

"Please! Stay with me, Valerie! I need you! I can't go on without you! I love you!" I cry even louder.

Valerie still doesn't speak, but her eyes show me all the love she has for me. Fear mixed with calmness are reflected in her gaze like she's ready to let go. Her hand drops, and she leans her head back into my lap. I reach down and kiss her, and when I pull back, she takes her final breath.

Chapter Twenty-Four

11:05 AM

Tears roll down my face as I rock back and forth, holding my beautiful Valerie in my lap, hoping, praying, and begging she'll come back. Her eyes are still open, so I bring my fingers to her face and close them.

I have nothing. No one. Everything has been taken from me. Am I the last human on Earth?

I want so badly for that man to return with his rifle and finish what he started. Take me too. I have nothing to live for. My life with Valerie will never happen. We'll never be together like we dreamt.

There's an emptiness inside me, one I've never felt before, and I don't know what to do. I can't leave Valerie's body here, but at the same time, I don't want to give up. I don't want to accept that she's gone, but I'll have to. I'll have to go on and live on my own without her.

A faint noise comes to my ears, and I hope it is someone here to finish me off, but only leaves are rustling in the breeze. The warship is becoming less and less visible in the sky, and I realize it's moving. The noise grows louder, and only now do I realize someone's speaking. It's a Thorn's voice, but there's no one in sight.

"Attention, survivors of Earth, we're leaving your planet," the deep voice says. Glancing around, I don't see a TV on. How am I hearing this? Is it in my head? "As you might have figured out, we were not just here to collect resources. The entire time we were here, we were watching your every move. Our race doesn't have a planet we call home anymore. We travel from planet to planet and do what we did here. Eventually, we will have conquered each planet with intelligent life. Then we will move on to the next galaxy and do the same. For your planet, we decided to leave behind one percent of the population to rebuild. We already disposed of the humans that were killed for you. Whether or not you come together after this is up to you. Lastly, we've chosen one person. This person has lost everyone they've ever known. The chosen one will receive the last orb, but there's a catch. This orb can either be used to reshape the world, make it a better place, or bring back someone they've lost. Only this person will know where to find it. We wish you luck."

I look up just as the warship disappears into the sky. Even with one percent of humans left, that's still a lot of people. How can we even possibly find out who this person is? But maybe there isn't someone and I imagined it. How could I have heard a broadcast when I'm nowhere near a TV and nobody's around me? But I know I didn't imagine it.

It's as if my body has a mind of its own when I gently set Valerie's body down and stand. I look around, and I now realize why this neighborhood looked so familiar before. Right in front of me is a small one-story house made of wood and painted yellow. I recognize it from a picture Mom had shown me once. Just like the picture, there's a pink mailbox in the yard with a small handprint on its side.

I walk up the pathway and up the wooden front porch. They don't make houses this small anymore, and the only reason it's still here is because the space it's taking up isn't enough to build anything bigger. So its sat here for years, abandoned. The front door is unlocked when I try to open it and step inside.

The inside is even smaller than the outside. The kitchen is the first room, with outdated tiles and wallpaper in an ugly shade of green. To the left is the one and only bedroom, with the ensuite bathroom. The living room is on the other side of the kitchen but is empty like the rest of the house. Except for the stove in the kitchen.

I walk into the bedroom, open the closet, and find a small wooden box. I crouch in front of the box and lift the lock. All four numbers are on zero, but somehow, I know exactly where they need to be. I change the number to 0816, and the lock clicks open.

When I open the box, a layer of dust falls off the top and makes a pile on the carpet. A light green glow comes from inside the box. A sphere, no bigger than a marble is hovering in the center. The orb is much brighter than the one I found, and it crackles with energy. I now realize why I was spared so many times. They chose me. But why?

When I grab the orb, I feel the world start to drift away as a vision appears before me. I see the leader of the Thorn like we're in the same room. He stares into my eyes, grinning, and I ball my fists.

"Hello, Lylon," he says, his voice deeper than ever.

"You know me?" I ask through gritted teeth.

We're surrounded by darkness and fog. The leader towers over me, at least three feet taller.

"Of course I know who you are. We've been studying the Earth for decades. You were chosen before we even invaded." His deep voice echoes all around me, making him even louder.

"Why me? What's so special about a normal teen?" I ask, genuinely curious. He grins even more, and I realize I'm biting my lip too hard.

"Your mother—"

"What does my mom have to do with any of this? You took her from me!" I say. The leader looks away for a moment and chuckles. He pulls his hand up, and an object appears on his palm. It looks like a snow globe. Inside is the surface of the Earth, but also a figure that looks like a human. The human bangs against the glass, and as I look closer, I gasp at the sight before me.

"Mom! Give her to me, now!"

"Your mother was the first human we encountered when one of our scout ships crashed to the surface. She was on a hike, seventeen years old at the time. We weren't ready to invade yet and saw no point in killing her. But we had to make sure she wouldn't spread the news. We told her if she kept quiet, all would be fine. She then became the most selfless person on the planet. Funny how that works."

Mom had encountered the Thorn all those years ago? She never mentioned it or even looked like anything was wrong. How could she keep that from me? Did Dad know? Now I realize what she meant when she always said she had to help others. She believed the Thorn would leave if she did.

"We know what choice your mother would make, even if she lost everyone, including you."

"You know nothing!" I scream. I almost lunge forward to smack the grin off his face, but then I remember we're in my head.

"Ahh, but we both know that's not true. Didn't you wonder why everyone was taken from you? How else do you think I killed everyone you ever knew?"

"You act all-powerful, but you don't have control over everything!"

Once again, he grins, showing his bottom fangs. "Hmm… Didn't I?"

"My… Dad," I say in a low voice.

"I sent that man because he proved he'd stop at nothing to achieve his goal. He didn't think twice when he took the orb, even though you got there first."

I now realize how much control the Thorn have had this entire time. The people around me who disappeared or got killed were all part of this monster's plan. The Thorn leader figured out everyone I knew and took them from me. He even sent the man who killed Dad. But Valerie?

"You also controlled the man who shot Valerie."

"That's right. Mind control is an interesting power to possess. I controlled his mind, and when I was done, I no longer needed him."

"This whole thing was the test."

"You see this medallion around my neck? It's a souvenir from my last battle. See, we never planned to return to our planet. It was never about the resources either. Our race travels to planets with intelligent life, defeats them, then leaves for the next planet. I like to take something from planets we conquer as a souvenir. Like this medallion, your mother is our souvenir from Earth. Don't worry. She'll be safe with me. We now have just one more planet in this galaxy before we move to the next," he says proudly.

"So, you just kill other races for sport?" I ask, disgusted.

"Look at us! Our race was made for this! We were made to conquer and destroy. But you humans… your ability to love and genuinely care about others is the reason we decided to test you. And now, you have a choice to make. Are you as selfless as your mother? Reshape humanity or bring someone back. It is up to you."

Everything goes black again until I'm back in the room. Finally, I know what to do, and I don't care if I fail the Thorn's stupid test. Nobody should be in a position to make this decision. I get up quickly and rush outside, collapsing next to Valerie. Without hesitating, I bring the orb up to my lips and begin to whisper.

"I wish I had Valerie back," I say.

The glow from the orb instantly cuts off as it turns to dust and rises into the sky. I wait, but nothing happens. Was this a joke? I continue to wait, but still, nothing happens. I put my ear on her chest, but I can't hear her heartbeat. Closing my eyes, I begin to sob.

Valerie might not come back.

Chapter Twenty-Five

Valerie

All I see is white.

Everywhere I look is just empty white space, and I have no idea how I got here. The last thing I remember is Lylon kissing me before the world went black. The pain I had is gone, and I can breathe again. It feels like a weight has been lifted off my shoulders. I look down at myself, but I can see through me. I still have color, but my hands and arms are a little transparent, like a ghost.

Am I dead?

Two shadows approach from the white fog. One is a foot taller than the other, but I can see who they are as they get closer. The woman is short with long blonde hair and blue eyes. Her skin is clear, and she has on a long purple dress. The man is bald with a patchy beard. He has hazel eyes and wears a white dress shirt with the top button undone.

"Mom! Dad!" I shout, racing toward them. They stop me before I can reach them, though.

"Valerie. We can't hug you. We're not here for that," my dad says.

I feel a little sad, but it doesn't matter because they're here. They smile at me, and it brings a smile to my own face. I never thought I would see them again, but I'm so happy they're here now.

"What is this place? Are we dead?" I ask. My parents look at each other and chuckle.

"Yes, Val, we're all dead," Dad says.

"So, is this heaven?"

Mom shakes her head. "Not quite. More like a gateway."

"We want you to know that we love you, and we'll always be with you, in here," Dad says and brings his fingers to his heart.

"But we're together. Am I not coming with you?"

"No, sweetie, you aren't."

"But I'm ready, and I want to be with you."

"And we want you to be with us, but someone else needs you," Dad says.

I close my eyes as realization sinks in. "Lylon!"

"That's right. What do you remember?" Dad asks.

"We were running from the Thorn downtown. Well, first, they brought us downtown, but that's a different story. Anyway, we were running and entered a neighborhood. Lylon stopped because his knee is super jacked up, and when we resumed walking, a man shot me with a rifle. Then I just remember falling into Lylon, and everything went black after he kissed me." My parents smile with their eyebrows raised. "What?"

"Why do you think you are returning?" Mom asks.

"I don't know. Are you going to tell me?" I ask, but everything finally clicks. "He used an orb on me?"

"That's right."

"But how? They were all used up, weren't they?"

"Yes, they were. The first ones, that is," Dad says. "But when the Thorn left, they gave one to someone they chose. This chosen person is somebody who lost everyone they ever knew. That was Lylon. He used the orb about ten seconds ago."

"But this orb was different. It could be used like the others, or it could've been used to reshape the world."

"And he chose me?" I ask.

Mom nods. "The love you two share is special. We can both see it, you know."

"So, am I just going to go back then? How does this work?"

"You will. But first, we have to tell you goodbye," Dad says.

"I don't want to say goodbye. But I do want to return to Lylon."

"Val… we are so proud of you, and we love you more than you could ever imagine. But you can't come with us. You need to return to Lylon. He has a big task at hand, and you need to help him."

"Tell Lylon he has my blessing," Dad says with a chuckle.

"I will."

I want to cry, but no tears come out. I actually feel refueled as I look at my parents for the last time. This is goodbye until I die for a second time. They both smile at me, and I smile back. I want this moment to last longer, but it already fades.

"I'm so sorry this happened to you."

"Don't be," Dad says and takes Mom's hand. "It's okay. We're okay."

"I love you both so much."

"And we love you unconditionally."

They smile once more and then fade completely.

I expect to return immediately, but I don't. Instead, I'm left for a moment surrounded by white fog. I miss my parents already, but I'm eager to see Lylon and tell him I love him. I want to marry him and start a family together. At that moment, everything turns super bright.

"Here I come, Lylon."

Chapter Twenty-Six

Lylon

My head still rests on Valerie's chest, waiting for any sign of her return. The orb should have worked. It had to. If it doesn't work, this is a sick joke.

I've lost everyone, and to give me false hope like that is just wrong. I know how cruel the Thorn are, but this is too low even for them.

A faint sound comes to my ears, and I stop breathing.

Thump, thump, thump.

The faint vibrations of her heart come from beneath her ribcage. I pull my head up as Valerie's body begins to shake. I lift her shirt, and the wound expands as the bullet lodged into her stomach rises out of her body. The bullet reaches the surface, and I take it off her body and hold it in my hand. The wound starts to stitch itself closed as it grows together, the tissue interlocking with one another. Tracing my fingers over the recently healed wound, it's completely smooth like it had never been there.

I put my ear to her heart, and the beat grows stronger and stronger. Color returns to her cheeks, and she looks so peaceful, as if she's sleeping. Valerie's eyes flutter open, and it takes her a moment before she meets my gaze. Tears form in my eyes as a smile returns to my face. This time, they aren't tears of despair, but of joy.

"You—you saved me," Valerie says, her voice weak.

"I can't live without you."

Valerie smiles back at me and closes her eyes, but this time I'm not afraid. She's not going anywhere. She needs to rest, we both do.

I pick her up, and her head falls into my chest. My knee burns from the added weight, but I don't care. I start to walk back the way we came, not a worry in the world. The Thorn have left, and we're it. There aren't any dangers left.

Only one place comes to mind I could go to right now. The hospital. They should have plenty of supplies to patch my wounds, and they'll have beds for us to rest. Thankfully, the hospital is only a block away.

I walk past the damaged buildings and wrecked cars until the hospital comes into view. Such a vast difference from the memory I had in my mind. Two wrecked ambulances are strewn near the entrance, and the sign is off. As I approach, the front door opens, and a short lady in a nurse's uniform with her hair pulled back in a low bun rushes toward us. She looks familiar.

"What happened?" she asks.

"We're good now. She just needs rest," I say as we enter the hospital.

"What about you?"

"My knee is badly bruised, but other than that, I'm fine. A brace helped, nothing that a good rest can't fix."

Since I know my way around here, I take Valerie to one of the rooms to my left, and the woman starts to examine her.

"How do you know so much about injuries?" she asks.

"My mom… she uh… she was a nurse. She worked here." The nurse pauses for a moment and looks me up and down, then smiles.

"Lylon?"

"Yeah… how'd you know?"

"I'm Janice. I worked with your mom. She often talked about you. Actually, your dad was here yesterday with a dog. How is he?"

"He briefly mentioned you before… before he uh was killed."

"Oh! I'm so sorry," Janice says and envelopes me in a hug.

***

I'm waiting in the lobby as the time passes by.

Despite my protests, Janice examined me and found that a bullet had grazed my side. The pain never registered, and no matter how hard I tried, I couldn't recall an incident where I could've been hit. I don't remember the guy who shot Valerie taking another shot. Maybe he did, and I was just too focused on Valerie to notice. Janice stopped the bleeding and stitched it up, then taped gauze over it. She also gave me an ice pack for my knee, and I've been holding it there for about half an hour. Closing my eyes, I rest my head against the wall. I want to see Valerie, but Janice is in there making sure everything is alright, and I have to give them some privacy.

Thankfully, a few minutes later, Janice emerges from the left hallway with a plate in hand. I never thought a peanut butter and jelly sandwich would give me such pleasure. It's something normal, familiar.

Janice sits next to me. "She's fine, just needs to rest."

"Thank you so much for everything."

"It's what I'm here for," she responds. "Do you mind me asking what happened to you two?"

"There's too much to tell. I wouldn't know where to start."

"We have a while. It might help pass the time," she says.

"Shortly after my dad passed, we found this group run by the mayor, but the Thorn found us and brought us downtown. The leader was down there offering us another orb, but a man pulled a gun and tried to shoot the leader. Like an avalanche, things escalated fast, and almost everyone was slaughtered there. Valerie and I ran, and here we are."

I don't want to tell her about using the orb on Valerie. I don't regret my decision, but I had the opportunity to do something great for the world, and I didn't take it.

"So, there are others then?" she asks.

"No. We're the only ones that made it," I answer. "Did they not come for you?"

"They made me stay here, but I didn't know why until now. I think I'm supposed to help others," she says.

"Well, you've helped us, so that's got to count for something, right?"

"Maybe."

***

After talking to Janice, I walk into Valerie's room. She had offered me a separate room so I could sleep, but I want to be next to Valerie when she wakes up. She's lying on her back and, just like always, looks so peaceful she sends all my nightmares away. I pull up a chair and sit next to her. I take her hand and kiss it before I rest my head on the bed and drift to a dreamless sleep.

Chapter Twenty-Seven

Morning

The first thing I see when I open my eyes is Valerie. She's still fast asleep, but I'm sure she'll wake up soon. I hear a light pitter-patter of rain on the window. The clock on the wall reads 7:05 AM. The last time I remember is 2 PM. Have we been sleeping for the past seventeen hours?

My mind goes to the invasion three days ago, and an involuntary shudder ripples through my body. I'm so glad it's finally over.

Valerie takes a deep breath and stirs. Despite sleeping that long I feel groggy. My neck hurts from sleeping in a chair, but my knee feels better, and the new brace Janice gave me helped a lot.

"Good morning, sleepyhead," I say to Valerie as she opens her eyes. She smiles at me and touches my hand.

"Good morning, beautiful," she replies.

I chuckle. "That's my line."

"You didn't use it."

"Touché."

"My dad gives you his blessing," she says, grinning.

"Huh?"

"When I passed, I saw my parents. My dad says you have his blessing."

"Oh, okay." Valerie looks at me expectantly, and that's when realization dawns on me. "Valerie?"

"Yes?"

"Will you make me the happiest man in existence and agree to spend the rest of your days with me? Valerie Ray…will you marry me?"

"Absolutely!" she says as an incandescent smile lights up her whole face.

"You may kiss the bride," I say with a deep voice before I crush my mouth on hers.

I don't know how long we kiss, but when we finally stop for air, I caress her soft skin, putting a stray strand of hair behind her ear.

"We need to find a pastor to make it official," she says.

"That might be a challenge, so until then, we are officially unofficially married."

An hour later, we get ready to leave. Janice hands me over a backpack with basic medical supplies, food and water.

Valerie hugs her. "Thank you for everything."

"You don't need to thank me," Janice says, looking at both of us.

"But we really do," I say.

"Well, if you ever need anything, I'll be here."

"We'll keep that in mind," I say. We give her a final smile, turn, and head out of the hospital.

Once again, I walk the empty streets with Valerie by my side, but this time, I don't worry about anything attacking us. I know I made the right choice with the orb. Life is full of selfish choices, and I'm prone to making them. But that will be the last selfish act I commit.

The rain has stopped, and the clouds have parted, leaving behind the sun and a rainbow. It's a nice cool morning, and the birds' melodic chirping brings a smile to our faces.

Valerie stops, takes a deep breath, and stretches in the warmth of the sunlight. "It's like Noah's ark all over again."

"Yeah," I say.

Valerie places her hands on her hips and looks at me. "So…what now?" she asks, but there's only one answer to her question.

"Now we change the world."

Epilogue

On a chilly day outside the White House, a crowd cheers for the man at the podium. He stands in a suit with a blue tie, with his long black hair tied in a bun. The crowd holds signs with the man's face and slogan, *Let's Rebuild the World!* Banners of red, white, and blue, as well as the American flag, hang everywhere.

The man on the wooden stage smiles at the crowd. Perhaps he's happy for the support, or he might be excited about his speech. The ecstatic crowd grows quiet as the man raises his hand. Taking a sip of his water, he greets them.

"Good morning, citizens of America! Today is a special day, but a sad one too. Today marks the 50th anniversary of the Thorn invasion. Today we remember all those who lost their lives at the hands of the Thorn. Today we remember how our lives changed forever. Today we remember those men and women brave enough to put up a fight so that the rest of us could live and fight another day. Today we remember how we had to start rebuilding our world.

Today is a tough day.

We knew we would face many hardships after that day fifty years ago. Despite the Thorn leaving, we knew people wouldn't immediately come together and become a big happy family. But we have been working hard, and just last year, we reached our first billion in world population since the Thorn invasion," the man pauses as more cheers fill the crowd. As they die down, the man continues his speech.

"I didn't live through the invasion, but I want to personally thank all of those who did. Because without you, we wouldn't be here. Thank you for your bravery, your wit, and your will to survive."

More cheers fill the crowd. The man takes another sip of water.

"I want to share a story with you all. Both of my parents lived through the invasion, but this story is about my father. During the invasion, he was given a choice. See, he had lost everyone he'd ever known. Everyone around him died: his parents, his friends, his newly adopted dog, and his future wife. He had lost everything. But the leader of the Thorn gave him the last orb. This final orb had no conditions. He could've guaranteed world peace, gotten rid of our growing threat of global warming, or extinguished world hunger for good because we still face similar problems to this day… Or he could've brought back someone he lost. I guess without his choice, I wouldn't be here talking to you today.

Ever since his choice he set out to make sure his decision was the right one. He vowed to never be selfish again, to look out for other people's interests before his own. He began to do what his mother did before him, caring for others beyond himself. He became a leader for the rebuilding process. And he has accomplished great things. We wouldn't be standing here today if it weren't for him and his efforts. But was it enough? We still face the same issues that we faced before the invasion. We still have threats of terrorism and war. We still have climate change. There are still places in the world not able to have a fresh supply of water. Crime still floods the streets. The world is much the same, there's just less people in it.

My father had the opportunity to achieve something bigger than himself, to make the world perfect, but he couldn't at the time. All choices have a price, and he couldn't bear the price of choosing the world. Even though he learned from his choice, and became a better man, the world is not better than it was before the invasion. It may never be. I want you all to think about that. If you had been in his shoes, what choice would you have made? As we all go about our daily lives on this day, as we take in all of the progress we have made, I want to leave you with a question. And going forward, I want you all to ask yourselves this same question every day…

Am I willing to bear the price of choices made to create a better world?"

About the Author

Joseph Noll is an American author who grew up in a city outside of Dallas, TX. When he was in the third grade, he was diagnosed with dyslexia and placed into Multisensory Teaching Approach classes. Despite facing these difficulties, Noll knew he had to overcome them to be successful going forward. With the support of his parents and teachers, he was able to overcome dyslexia and no longer needed the extra assistance going into the fifth grade. Although Noll overcame his struggles, he continued to hate reading and writing until that changed when he reached high school. By sophomore year, Noll had many ideas swirling inside his mind but still refused to commit to one of them. Finally, during his senior year, he decided to sit down and begin writing his first novel, The Thorn, at the age of 17.